A Prophecies of Angels and
Demons Novella

Firefly

Book 1.5

CASSANDRA ASTON

If you were looking for a happy ending, stop reading now

CONTENT &TRIGGER WARNINGS

This book is a work of fiction. No part of this book should be construed as true or accurate; no people or animals were harmed in the creation of this story. Firefly is intended for mature readers and recommends 18+. Mature content and triggers are listed below.

Descriptions of torture and death

Descriptions of family tragedy and mental and physical torture

References to war, experimentation, and starvation

Necromancy and reincarnation

Biblical and other related references

References to angels, demons, heaven, hell, and consequences for human actions

Explicit language

Witches, magic, and other magical, fantastical beings

CONTENTS

PROLOGUE
1941

I died. I'm dead. The thought ran through his mind again, though he hadn't dared utter the words aloud. But those were the words he wanted to tell her, to make her understand he hadn't left by choice, that he never would have left her.

When she looked at him with such fear, such blind terror, he knew a part of her must already understand.

He took a step toward her, but she flung out her hand, a gust of wind knocking him back.

"Don't come near me!"

"Rebecca, I know what you must think, but it's not..."

Her eyes darted to the two small boys behind him.

"Come here, boys. Quickly." The quiver in her voice was slight, but he recognized it for what it was, knew it as he knew his own soul, and something fractured inside him at the condemnation in her words.

He had been reunited with the woman he loved, even if only by chance, and she had found him wanting.

When she left, taking the boys with her (never turning her back on him), all that remained were his doubts. He turned, fleeing into the night. He didn't care where he went or why—to stay and face the truth would be far worse.

CHAPTER 1

Simon

1942

Simon ducked behind a branch, cursing as his father leaned out his bedroom window, peering into the night.

Humans couldn't see the way his eyes glowed in the dark, but Simon never stopped fearing one would see what he truly was—a monster.

Since he'd died and come back in this new form, he'd only been to see his father once. He had intended to lie, to tell his father he was still alive in hopes of assuaging some of his grief, but when he'd gone to his family home, it had been empty.

It took two months of searching to learn his father was living in Elizabeth City, working for the coast guard, and another three months to work up the courage to seek him out.

Now, he wondered if it was too late.

At first, Simon had been reported as a deserter until a body turned up and was identified by Alexander, his former employer—current employer, even if he was no longer paid.

It wasn't Simon's body. *His* body had been buried in one of the unmarked graves on the estate. It was just another of Alexander's hapless victims, and no one would question the wealthiest man in town when he said the body that washed ashore—bloated and disfigured—was Simon Carey's.

His father ducked his head, slid the window closed, and drew the curtains.

Simon jumped down from his perch, dusting his pants free of residual leaves or tree bark, and ran his fingers through his hair. He hadn't cut it since his death; hadn't needed to. The new transformation had somehow frozen him in time.

Would his father notice he hadn't aged?

He raised a hand to the door, curling his fingers into a fist when the sound of laughter froze him in place. It was a woman's laugh, high and tinkling, and his father's chuckle followed shortly after.

He leaned closer, listening. Music played softly, and the woman giggled again.

Moving beside the kitchen window, he darted a look inside. His father was dancing. With a woman.

Simon leaned against the wall of his father's temporary housing, taking deep breaths. His father was dancing and... laughing. He'd never thought his father would do any of those things again after his mother died, and certainly not after the death of his only son.

He risked another peek through the window. They were swaying in unison, her head resting on his shoulder. Something in Simon's chest swelled.

He slouched against the wall, a smile forming on his lips as their soft voices filled some of the hollow space inside him. His father was happy. Who was he to take that away from him?

Pushing off the wood at his back, Simon darted into the darkness. With any luck, he could make it back to the Graves estate without Alexander ever realizing he'd left. The less Alexander knew about his personal affairs, the better.

3

He stopped at the fence surrounding the estate and slipped through the gap he'd made between two posts. The iron was for show. Only the gargoyles, situated every few posts and glaring out into the night, protected them from the demons scouring the Earth in search of dark deeds and darker souls.

Passing through each night eased his conscience. If he were evil, surely the gargoyles would have barred his entry.

He dashed between the saplings and mature apple trees to the back of the Graves mansion and cracked the door, moving on silent feet down the servant's corridor, past his room, and into the kitchen, where he settled himself in a chair, fingers drumming on the wood counter.

He wanted to resume his relationship with his father, but it was a selfish wish, born of a desire to cling to the only family he had left. His father deserved to move on with his life and find solace where he could. The world believed Simon was dead. Perhaps he was, and it would be best for everyone if he remained that way.

CHAPTER 2

Rebecca

It was late when Sarah had finally gone down after a fitful night of tossing and turning. Rebecca needed tea or a heavy pour of whiskey, but her father kept the alcohol locked up as if she were still a child.

To risk asking him hardly seemed worth the trouble. These days when he deigned to acknowledge her existence, it was because he wanted something from her. More often than not, her magic.

It was a dirty bit of narcissism that made her father this way. He coveted what he could not have and made others around him pay for all the ways he was lacking. Rebecca's greatest sin had been being born with more magic than her father, and for that, he sought to punish her. And find a way to claim it.

If she could have left, taken Sarah, and gone anywhere else, she would have, but with no money and no one to care for them, she was as trapped on the estate as she had been as a child.

James had been her one chance to escape, and even he hadn't wanted her in the end.

Still, she would do it all again for Sarah. Sarah was her reason for living, her only hope for some small bit of joy. For Sarah, she would endure anything, even her father's experimentation.

Once, she had dreamed of a life with Simon. He was kind and good, and he loved her, but he'd fallen victim to her father's greed—as they all eventually did. Now, he was her father's henchman, carrying out whatever illicit deeds needed doing in the dark.

She might have forgiven him his indiscretions if he'd come to her, told her. Instead, he'd left one night, too cowardly to tell her the truth.

When she'd found him in the orchard, bringing those boys to her father, her heart had shattered. Perhaps it was luck that took her outdoors that fateful night. Had she not seen with her own eyes, she may never have believed her father when he told her Simon had agreed to work for him.

Rebecca stepped through the door to the kitchen and froze, hand going to her chest.

"Simon," she breathed. "You scared me."

What were the odds? She'd just been thinking of him, and he was there in the kitchen after so many months. Well, better than she'd like to admit if she were being honest—she thought of him often.

"So you're back," she said, moving past him to the sink to fill a glass of water. She kept her back to him, gathering her composure.

"Yes."

The sadness in that one word had her turning around. She searched his face, looking for any sign of the killer her father had described, the ruthless man who had chosen money and a life of crime over her. But in his eyes, there was only heartbreak and a darkness that had never been there before.

Her chest ached, and she longed to go to him—wrap her arms around him—and ask him why he seemed so changed, but bitterness hung between them. Bitterness and regret.

She cleared her throat. "You've been gone a while. I wasn't sure you were coming back."

He tensed, the muscles along his arms tightening as he slid his chair back and stood.

She clenched her cup, some instinct telling her there was danger here.

"I hope you're well," he said, moving glacially toward her as if he knew any sudden movement might scare her away.

She dipped her chin, throat too dry to form a response.

"And Sarah?"

She swallowed. "It was her birthday today."

"That's great." His smile was forced, and it turned the knife already buried in her chest.

"You've been gone for half a year."

"Not by choice," he whispered, inching closer as she leaned back into the counter behind her.

Her words were barely a breath as she asked: "Were you forbidden from seeing us?"

"No—"

That single word brought her fiery temper raging back. Or perhaps it was her only defense against the loneliness and rejection rising in her. "My father told me everything, so don't bother lying."

She had given Simon all of herself—her body, her heart—and he had left without a word. Some small part of her had prayed Alexander was lying, but in the end, he had been right. No one cared for her. No one would ever love her.

She tucked her fractured heart back into its dark corner and resolved to give him the honesty he didn't deserve.

"We missed you, Simon. *I* missed you."

It wasn't meant as anything but truth. Perhaps she hoped if she gave him a bit of honesty, he would do the same.

He closed the last bit of distance between them, saying nothing, and she steadied herself for the blow. His truth would cut deep, but she had to hear it; she had to know it was always one-sided so she could move on with her life.

He raised one hand and froze, a question in his eyes.

She lifted her chin. "I'm not afraid of you."

A lie.

After she'd just promised herself she would give him the truth. But perhaps the lie was for herself because, in this moment, nothing terrified her more than what she knew would come next.

His hand closed over hers, and gently, he pried her fingers from the cup, kissing each one as he did.

She sucked in a breath.

"I won't hurt you," he said, and she tasted the truth of his words.

"I know."

He set the cup down beside her and pulled her toward him. She let him, not daring to breathe as his head tilted to the side, his nose grazing the side of her cheek.

Warm breath caressed her ear as he said, "I've missed you more than you could imagine."

CHAPTER 3

Simon

He inhaled her scent. It was sweet, rose petals dripping with morning dew, and it was heaven. He buried his face in her hair, releasing one hand to let his fingers trail down the soft fabric at her back.

Shocks of electricity danced between the fabric of her robe and his skin. In their wake, waves of desire followed. In that moment, he wished for nothing more than her body pressed against his—flesh against flesh. And as if his thoughts were mirrored in her own, a mad frenzy overtook her as she pulled at her robe, revealing pale, creamy skin.

He released her, moving a breath away, and she stopped undressing, her eyes meeting his as her glazed expression cleared.

She stumbled back into the counter, her pulse thrumming wildly. "What... What did you do?"

It took a moment for his own mind to clear and the words to sink in. She was blaming him for her sudden desire.

"I didn't..." he faltered.

Her hand went to her chest. "Please, let me go."

He stepped back, giving her space, and she slid around him, backing toward the door.

"Rebecca."

She glanced behind her. "I should check on Sarah."

He nodded, and she continued backing up.

Something in her expression had changed. The woman who had barricaded herself inside the house six months before was back and was no less frightened of him now than she had been that night in the orchard with those two small boys.

He watched her go, saying nothing. He had been wrong to push her. Perhaps she wasn't ready for this version of him; perhaps she never would be. He waited, hoping for just a moment she might come back, change her mind, and throw herself into his arms.

When she didn't return, he left the kitchen, following the hall to the stairs that led to Alexander's laboratory. He dreaded going, but if he didn't check in, Alexander would come looking for him, and that was never a good thing.

The room was bathed in an unnatural light as the amulet swung from some imaginary string, glowing faintly. Alexander wasn't there, but he couldn't be far. He never left the necklace for long.

As if on cue, the door leading up the back stairs swung wide, and Alexander strode in.

He was a tall man, even compared to Simon, standing at least two inches taller and carrying himself with an air of importance that only lent to his height.

"You're back. Good. I have work for you."

Simon dipped his head, hiding his scowl. It was a blessing. He would be allowed to leave and be far from Alexander. He had to remind himself of this fact every time Alexander gave him a new and terrible task.

"I need more demons. Rebecca grows weaker by the day. You must find me more. Preferably ones with stronger essences. The last were weak, barely enough to sustain her strength for days."

It was a lie. One Alexander fed him every time he wanted Simon to bring back demons. One Simon pretended to believe to ensure he didn't find himself shackled to the ceiling in the dark room where Alexander performed his magic.

"I leave for New York tonight."

Alexander met his gaze, his penetrating stare boring into Simon's as if to eke out any deception. When he found none, he smiled. "Good."

Simon turned to leave. He would check in on Rebecca and Sarah, ensure they were safely tucked away in their beds, and then he would leave this house and the memory of Rebecca's horror-stricken face.

With distance between them, he could admit something strange had happened when they touched. He couldn't say what, but whatever it was, she was convinced it had been his fault.

He had acquired other gifts in his new form: speed, enhanced hearing, and canines that lengthened at will. Was it such a leap to assume he might possess other yet undiscovered gifts?

"Oh, and Simon," Alexander said to his back, "take Astaroth with you."

He ground his teeth, stalking from the room.

CHAPTER 4

Rebecca

Rebecca slid between soft sheets, letting the fabric chill her overheated skin. Shocks of electricity still sparked in her veins along her back where Simon's fingers had brushed down her spine. She pressed her fingers to her throbbing pulse at the base of her neck, and her breath caught, remembering the way she'd pictured him taking her there on the kitchen counter.

She took a steadying breath and leaned over the side of her bed to peer into Sarah's crib.

Although the baby had her own room, Rebecca never felt comfortable leaving her all alone across the hall in their large home.

She smiled down at her sweet baby as pale cheeks, illuminated by the moon's silvery glow, puffed before exhaling another deep breath. Dropping her head into the crib, she pressed a kiss to Sarah's forehead and inhaled her sweet scent.

Some of the tension racketing her body eased as she leaned back and fell onto her pillows.

She stared up at a pink ceiling, wondering how the evening might have gone had she only given in to the feelings coursing through her. But Simon had left her, chosen her father's money without even saying goodbye. She would not be that girl—the girl who threw herself at a man who clearly had an interest in only one thing.

He'd gotten what he wanted, and no matter how real it felt, it was clear she meant nothing to him.

A shudder stole through her as the hairs on the back of her neck prickled. A foretelling feeling that something was coming. *Change.*

Her premonitions were never wrong. This one told her that her life was soon to be altered—and not for the better. Her health had been slowly deteriorating, and thanks to her father's ministrations, the drain seemed to be hastening her demise.

The doctors had told her she was dying. A rare illness that had no cure. They could not say *when* she would die, only that it would be before her time. And that it may come suddenly.

True to their word, each month, she felt as though she had aged a decade. At twenty-three, she felt closer to sixty, but just one year prior, she'd felt as though she were in her thirties, and the year before that, she'd nearly felt invincible. It was as though being told she would die had signaled her body to start the process of deterioration.

She could only imagine what she might feel like another year from now—if she were still alive.

Rebecca exhaled sharply, watching one dark curl fly from her face and hover just overhead. It hung suspended in midair as she watched it, smiling.

She lifted a hand, caressing the breeze that sometimes accompanied her, and let the curl slide over her finger. Something in her chest buzzed in response, and she sighed, settling into her blankets.

Light streaked across her room as her door silently cracked open. She held her breath and closed her eyes.

Goosebumps pebbled her skin as the presence of something *other* entered the room. She'd felt it before when Simon crowded her space, and it left her feeling uneasy, but she couldn't place it.

Forcing her breathing to even out, she lay still, inhaling his lavender scent.

He was close, close enough that his soft scent overwhelmed her, but she let her lashes rest gently on her cheeks as she remained still.

Soft lips caressed her cheek, and she froze, breath catching in her throat. He was still there, hovering just over her, and she was sure he must know she was awake.

Another moment passed, and just as she was about to fling open her eyes, Sarah mumbled something in her sleep. His overwhelming presence moved, stepping back. He was silent. A wraith. But she knew when he left the room, could feel the moment he was gone.

Waiting several seconds, she exhaled a slow breath as her eyes fluttered open, darting around the room.

She peeked down at Sarah once more, whispering her thanks to the tiny cherub before kissing her again.

Blinking several times, her gaze fell on something glinting in the moonlight.

She got up, treading softly to the bookcase in the corner of the room, where she found a small ring and a note folded under it.

She tore the note open, reading:

Rebecca,

I owe you so much more than a letter of apology for my absence, and I long for the night when I'll be able to tell you these things in person. Please know I've thought of you, longed for you, and wished for nothing more than you by my side these many months.

As you know, my obligation to the army could only be broken by death or severe injury. Let me say only this on the subject. Your father found a way around both.

Though I dream of you and you alone, please understand that my debt to him is heavy. I could not ask you to bear this weight beside me, so I will keep my distance.

You deserve a lifetime of happiness with a man who can give you everything your heart desires.

Once, I believed myself capable of being that man. I see now it was never meant to be. I can only hope to one day regain your friendship and your trust.

With love,

Simon

Rebecca swiped at the hot tear streaking down her face and crumpled the letter, tossing it to the floor. She stalked to the door, threw it wide, and marched out into the hall.

A cool breeze caressed her cheek, urging her back under her covers. She ignored it, storming down the stairs.

She paused in the now-dark kitchen, listening for any sound that might give him away. When she was sure the room was empty, she left, trailing down the hall of windows to the set of rooms at the back of the house, and stopped in her father's study. It was empty, apart from stacks of journals balancing precariously atop one another.

Marching past the laundry room, her sister's old studio, and a guest bedroom, she stepped into the servant's wing and ran her hand along the wall, finding a switch and flipping it on. Dim yellow bulbs flared to life, illuminating the space every few feet in a soft yellow glow.

She stopped at the door to Simon's room and knocked.

In the silence that followed, she huffed out a breath and knocked louder.

"Don't ignore me, Simon."

When there was still no response, she pushed the door open, letting it swing wide.

The room was dark, his bed neatly made. A single sheet of paper lay in the corner where his writing desk sat.

Rebecca,

How can I explain?

The words were crossed out. Below them, he had started again.

Where can I start to tell you everything that has befallen me?

Those words were crossed out, too. After a few more scratched-out sentences, she scanned the page to the last words.

Please forgive me.

CHAPTER 5

Simon

Simon leaned into the shadows, listening. After more than a year of hunting, he knew where to find them. They scoured back alleys and dens of iniquity. Hovered outside brothel windows and near gambling clubs. Where the darkest denizens dwelled, that was where you would find demons.

A cool wisp of smoke leaned into his back, making his lip curl.

"Would you mind giving me space?" he growled.

Astaroth slid back, floating on a dank breeze. He wasn't close enough to touch Simon, but his presence drowned out the other demons in the area.

"I can't hunt if you're hovering."

Astaroth sighed dramatically and moved back several feet, giving Simon room to let his senses go to work.

The sound of fists pounding into flesh in a nearby gaming house, money clinking into a palm as bets were exchanged, and catcalls from the nearby brothel window melded into the cacophony of sounds drifting on the breeze.

A soft sniffle caught his attention, and he stilled. While he tended to fidget when idle, something predatory overtook his senses when prey was near.

His limbs went taut, every muscle coiling in preparation.

The sniffle came again, followed by a small moan, and the smell of sulfur grew stronger.

He sprang into action, moving at a speed even a demon couldn't outrun. In moments, he was on the dark thing, canines lengthening as he tore through the partially corporeal form, finding the sweet essence below.

The demon gave a startled cry before she thrashed wildly, attempting to shake him off. He sucked harder, draining her, and in moments she dissolved into nothing, leaving only a woman lying crouched against the wall.

She looked up, terror in her dark eyes.

"It's alright. You're safe now," he said, holding out a hand. She flinched back, and he knew without looking that Astaroth had arrived. "He can't harm you while I'm here."

She cast her gaze over his shoulder at the insidious creature at his back.

He turned, showing Astaroth his teeth, and the demon backed up, hissing. He stalked toward him, backing them out of the alley.

Astaroth raised both hands, his form dissolving around the edges. "Sssimon, Alesssander will be disssspleased if I tell him of your heroicsss."

Simon smiled, letting his sharp teeth glint in the lamplight. "Not if I drain you first."

Astaroth went translucent, only his face and arms still visible. "I would be back eventually."

Simon's smile widened. "I never tire of imagining ways to end you."

Astaroth dissolved into the shadow along the wall. "Sssave her, but don't think I won't tell Alesssander."

Simon turned, not waiting for the demon to say more, and rushed back to the woman leaning into the wall, holding her side. He wrapped an arm around her waist gently and pulled her up.

She stiffened under his touch but didn't pull away.

They moved through the darkened street in silence. Although her gait was slow, the limp heavily pronounced, she never said a word, resolute in her determination, until they reached a cracked, wooden door.

What began as shaking hands quickly morphed into tremors that racked her small frame.

Simon's mood darkened. He'd thought the demon had been the one to injure her in that dark alley, but her terror after all she had endured spoke of a different kind of monster. He glanced down, truly looking at her.

She was little more than a girl, sixteen at most, and her clothes hung off her frame.

His grip tightened, and the tremors racking her body intensified.

He loosened his hold, working to get his emotions under control. He would get her to safety and return to deal with the monster.

"Do you trust me?" he whispered, knowing she had no reason to trust anyone in her life. She bit her lip and nodded. "Good."

It was all he said before he scooped her into her arms and darted into the night.

He stopped outside the Convent of the Sacred Heart and set the girl down beside him. She leaned into him, peering up at the gray spires stretching toward the inky sky. Her tremors had subsided, but she was breathing hard, her pulse thrumming in her veins.

The allure of that pulsing heartbeat was strong, reminding him of the taste of human blood. The way their essence felt rushing through him. Even those who had been infected by demon rot held such immense life.

Where demon essence curbed his craving for hours or, at best, a few days, a human's blood sated his desire for weeks. It felt different going down.

He swallowed against the thought, leaning away from the girl.

She slouched into him, unsteady on her feet.

"You'll be safe here. The nuns who run this convent will look after you," he said, giving her a gentle push forward.

She stumbled, catching herself before she fell, and took one step up the stone path before glancing back at him.

He nodded encouragingly, stuffing his hands into his pockets.

She knocked on the door, wrapping her arms tightly around herself. The door creaked, soft light spilling out. When she looked back, he was gone.

CHAPTER 6

Simon

Simon would be punished for helping the girl and draining the demon rather than bringing it back to Alexander, but it was a small price to pay if it chipped at his blackened soul. It was a typical night for him. These many months, he'd saved countless poor souls from demons of all kinds, but he always ended the night with a catch.

He would drag the demon back to Alexander, and Alexander would begin the work of extracting its essence to prolong his own life.

He always sent Simon away for that part, explaining they were meant for Rebecca—to save her. But she was weaker each time he saw her, while Alexander only seemed to grow more youthful and vibrant.

Simon had learned the truth on a night when Alexander had been too caught up in his casting to notice the creature lurking in the corner, watching. He had tried everything to escape the hold Alexander had on him after that, but nothing worked.

The spells binding him were ironclad.

He stalked through the shadows, sensing the moment Astaroth reappeared. He wasn't sure how he knew Astaroth from the other demons. There was just something about him that was different. Once, when Simon had encountered a particularly strong demon, the signature was similar but not quite the same.

"Ssstill sssaving damsssels?" he hissed in Simon's ear.

Simon ignored the demon, tuning his senses to the night. It was just after two in the morning, and patrons were stumbling out of side doors and down walkways in droves, leaving the after-hours clubs. Some would head home, but others were intent on chasing the high.

Those were the men he was seeking.

A bawdy group who draped arms over each other's shoulders, slurring profanities, caught his eye. As the group turned off the main street, two inky shapes peeled themselves from the walls behind the men.

Simon waited until they were corporeal enough to sink his teeth into before he struck. He hooked the first between his fingers, biting into the second just enough to gain his full attention.

The first wriggled in his grip, working to get free, but the second, whose essence dribbled onto his tongue, froze. He wrapped his other arm around him, slowly letting his teeth retract enough to loosen his hold before biting into the first.

The demon caught in his arms dematerialized, freeing himself from Simon's hold, and Simon bit down on a curse as he latched onto the other.

When his nails or his teeth broke skin, something stopped the creatures from escaping. He wasn't sure why or how, but there were many things he didn't understand about his new life.

Like how Rebecca could look at him like she might still have some shred of feelings for him one moment, then race out of the room in terror the next. Or how, after so many months and his own death, she still consumed his thoughts every night.

Simon tugged the squirming creature in his arms—hooked through the shoulder by his nails—through the darkened streets, keeping his eyes peeled for any demons that might race to this one's aid.

It was rare, but it had happened on occasion.

In his new state, Simon no longer possessed the ability to heal from his wounds, caught somewhere between life and death. His body didn't age or weaken, but neither did it heal. He was faster and stronger than demons, but they were cunning devils who might gain the upper hand if they managed to sneak up on him.

He reached the outskirts of the city as the demon realized he wasn't in immediate danger and began a slew of curses aimed at Simon's character. Often, they were silent creatures when they weren't whispering deceit in human ears, and he wished this one had been the same.

When its droning had gone on longer than he could stand, he let his canines lengthen, opening his mouth in threat.

The demon's curses evaporated and were quickly replaced by pleas.

"Please, for the love of everything holy. Shut up," he groaned.

Safely outside the city and the eyes of humans, he burst into an unnatural run, digging his nails deeper into the demon's flesh. Green trickled down his fingers, whipping past him as he ran faster.

Of course, Astaroth had been no help. Rather than catching the second demon, he'd vanished, leaving Simon to do the dirty work.

Simon still marveled at never getting tired in his new form, even when he ran for hours. He'd once run most of the night, arriving just before dawn at his destination, and had no trouble catching his breath the moment he stopped at the edge of the beach in Monterey Bay. What might have taken weeks by train had taken him only one night.

It was his first time in California. It was his first time anywhere outside the East Coast. For just a moment, he'd imagined staying there forever, starting a new life for himself, but something tugged at his chest, calling him back to Bath, North Carolina, and the man who now owned him.

As the forest grew dense with oak and maple trees and the familiar scent of the North Carolina coastline assaulted him, he slowed. The demon in his grasp was suspiciously silent, and he turned the creature to face him, only to sigh in exasperation.

The demon's head listed to the side, his essence near depletion.

Simon huffed before biting into the creature and sucking the last of his essence dry. When nothing remained but the green ooze coating Simon's fingers, he sped the rest of the way to the estate.

Alexander would not be pleased.

CHAPTER 7

Rebecca

Rebecca set Sarah down on her favorite yellow blanket in a patch of grass where they might enjoy the dying embers of the sun's warmth before night fell.

Sarah cooed and giggled, rolling onto her back to stare up at the changing sky.

It was Rebecca's favorite time of day: when the world drank in the last rays of sun in preparation for night. As the sun set, the world was bathed in sepia tones, and only the bravest stars peeked out from behind fading clouds.

She reached up, picked an apple from the tree beside them, and bit into it, relishing the mix of bitter and sweet.

Relaxing back on the blanket, she sighed. It had been two nights since their encounter in the kitchen. Two nights since Simon had pressed a kiss to her cheek, left her a note, and vowed never to see her again.

After assuming him dead for half a year and spending another six months knowing he wasn't but hearing nothing from him, she was tired of letting him make all their choices. She believed he *had* found himself in some sort of trouble with her father, and it was just like her father to twist the situation to suit him.

Why had he chosen to exclude her from his life rather than enlist her help? Because he was a man.

Rebecca huffed out another breath.

Leaning back, she glanced over at Sarah and smiled.

Floating lazily overhead were a dozen semi-translucent butterflies. Tentatively, she stretched her finger toward the creatures and marveled as one popped as if it were a bubble made of dish soap.

Sarah's tiny body shook with laughter as she clapped her hands together in delight. Rebecca popped another of the butterflies, and something in her chest warmed as Sarah's laughter intensified.

When she had popped all the bubbles and the pair were red-cheeked from elation, she lifted the cherub into her arms and fluttered her lashes over her face.

"Rebecca. I need you."

A sliver of ice slid down Rebecca's spine. She fluttered her lashes over Sarah's skin again, using the time to school her features into calm. Had her father seen what Sarah could do? She'd hoped and prayed Sarah wouldn't have her gifts, wouldn't be another person he could use for his own ends.

It hadn't been the first time Sarah showed her abilities, and it wouldn't be the last. Rebecca felt time flying by at breakneck speed, and she was helpless to slow the inevitable end she knew was coming.

It was only a matter of time before Alexander learned Sarah had magic and used her, too. Until Rebecca had a better plan, she would let him take her own magic. When the time was right, she and Sarah would run. She only hoped her tired body would be able to keep up.

She moved past her father, into the house, and up the stairs. "I'm tired tonight, father. Could we do it tomorrow?"

Alexander's dark brows drew together, bunching at the bridge of his very long nose. "All the more reason to do so tonight, Rebecca."

She bit down on the inside of her cheek to keep from voicing her thoughts and kept walking. "Very well. I'll just put Sarah to bed."

She held her breath, waiting for him to disagree. When he said nothing, she continued up the stairs, her pace slower than the night before. When she reached her room, she set Sarah in her crib and laid a stuffed cat beside her.

"Go to sleep, my love. I will be back in a moment."

Sarah didn't protest; her large blue eyes only blinked up at Rebecca, too wise for her two years.

Rebecca hummed softly, a tune her older sister Margaret used to sing to her when she was very little.

Sarah's eyes fluttered, and she wrapped chubby fingers around the cat, a contented smile forming on her pink lips.

Rebecca pressed a kiss to her cheek and continued humming as she backed out the door. She turned and started as she nearly smacked into her father's lanky form just outside the door.

"You coddle the child. She'll be too soft when you're gone."

The words were a slap. A vicious reminder she was dying and Sarah would have no one in the world to care for her. Swallowing, Rebecca moved around her father, heading toward the stairs.

"Not that way. Let's take the back stairs," Alexander said from behind her.

She balled her fists at her sides but said nothing, turning to follow her father to his room and the staircase leading off of it that led to his secret underground room. In his bedroom, painted in horrid shades of red and black, her gaze darted to the bookshelf in the room's corner, untouched after so many years.

It was the one thing that hinted her father may have a heart buried somewhere deep within the folds of his vile chest.

She followed him into the room he'd built to hide most of his spell books and artifacts gathered on their family over the years.

Her father flipped a light switch on the wall and pulled a rope beside it to let Alice know they were going down. Rebecca wrapped her arms around herself tightly. Even with the dim illumination in the back stairs, she hated going down them, imagining she would tumble to her death every time.

Although her father had built a second set of stairs on the first floor, he seldom went that way, preferring to go between his bedroom and his secret underground room unnoticed.

No one in the family knew how much of his time he spent down there, but they all suspected it was a great deal of it.

At the bottom of the stairs, Alexander wasted no time moving to the center of the room and flipping open his journal filled with spells and the ramblings of their long-deceased family members.

"Come, Rebecca. Don't waste my time."

Rebecca moved stiffly, unable to keep memories of prior experiments from her mind as she reached the table and stood beside her father.

"I said don't waste my time," he snarled, gripping her arms tightly as he lifted her onto the table.

She held in a cry as she slid back, putting space between herself and her father. His grip would leave marks.

"Lay down."

She knew those words were coming, but some defiant part of her had wanted to make him say them, to prove to herself she wasn't at his mercy, no matter how untrue it might be.

She lay back, staring up at the darkened ceiling as Alexander lifted his amulet from around his neck and shot a ring of orange flame around it, suspending it overhead. The heat from his flame warmed her chest and lit the room.

As he began mumbling, Rebecca let her gaze wander, stopping on the gargoyles for a moment to wonder why he'd had the hideous things commissioned before deciding she didn't care what her father did. Something glinted in the dark, startling her: shackles hanging from the ceiling.

"No," she breathed as she took in the limp form hanging from them—swallowed by the darkness—chocolate locks obscuring his face from view.

CHAPTER 8

Simon

Simon groaned, blinking in the dark. As his eyes adjusted to the dim space, dread froze him, drowning out any minor aches.

Rebecca was bound and gagged, draped over her father's table. The one Simon had seen Alexander use dozens of times to strap down men and women as he pulled demons from them, killing them in the process.

A hundred different scenarios played out in his mind as he tried to imagine how this could have happened. A demon had possessed her; she had tried to run, and her father had stopped her. She had come down and found him chained to the ceiling and tried to save him...

If it were the last, he would die before he'd let her pay for him.

Rebecca moaned, her eyes fluttering open.

"Good. You're both awake. Let me tell you how this will go."

Simon tore his gaze from Rebecca's too-pale cheeks, glaring daggers at Alexander.

Reading the murder in his eyes, Alexander chuckled. "The two of you will do everything I ask. If one of you steps out of line, the other pays for it."

Rebecca moaned again, drawing Simon's gaze back to her. She was awake, but her eyes were unfocused. Whatever Alexander had done to her, she wasn't lucid. He wished for nothing more than to be free of his restraints and tear the head from Alexander's body, watching as his life drained from him.

Alexander moved between them, blocking Simon's view, and scowled, his jaw clenching tightly before he whispered something, raising his arms over his head and stepping back.

"Are you ready to listen, Rebecca?" It was a rhetorical question as she was still immobile on the table, mouth covered. But her eyes had cleared, and her focus rested wholly on her father, the hate simmering in her gaze, a mirror to Simon's own.

Alexander leaned over Rebecca, untying her gag and the ropes securing her wrists. He left her feet tied, motioning for her to sit up. She touched her lips, staring at the red smeared across her fingers, and darted a glance at Simon.

His vision had gone black at the edges, something feral begging to be released, to punish the man who had made her bleed, but no amount of pulling at his restraints would free him. They were spelled. Even a broken thumb wouldn't release him.

He writhed in anger, watching as Alexander instructed her to repeat his words. She did, never breaking eye contact with her father as she spoke. Alexander drew a small blade from the bag beside him and ran it down the length of her forearm.

Deep crimson welled along its path, bleeding over her fair skin before it ran down her arm, over the tip of her finger and into a bowl in Alexander's waiting hand. The bowl filled, and Alexander replaced it with a second, carelessly spilling her life force on the dirt floor as he took his time retrieving it from the same bag.

When the second bowl had filled, Rebecca swayed, and Simon's stomach dropped. "You'll kill her."

Alexander ignored him, digging through his bag for a third bowl. When he'd found it, he held it out, pressing either side of her cut to stimulate blood flow.

Simon thrashed in his chains uselessly, shouting in frustration, but Alexander ignored him even as Rebecca grew paler.

When the third bowl had filled, Alexander set it down, letting her blood drip onto the floor.

"You have what you want. Heal her. Would you kill your own daughter?" He sagged against his restraints, the ache in his chest overshadowing the one in his arms and shoulders.

Alexander turned slowly, taking his time. When their eyes met, something evil stared back at Simon. "Let this be a lesson. The next time I ask you to bring me a demon, do what you were made for rather than wasting your time saving riffraff."

Pain sliced through Simon's chest as he realized this torment was his fault and the woman on the table might die for it.

Rebecca swayed again, and Alexander turned, catching her. He set her head on the table but did nothing to stop the blood now dribbling over the side of it.

Simon looked between Alexander and Rebecca, whose lids were growing heavy. "I swear." The words were a whisper on his lips, a prayer to whatever god listened to save her.

Alexander chuckled. "Oh, no need to swear. I'll leave you with her as a reminder so that next time you're thinking of doing something reckless, the image of your lover will be burned into your retinas."

Not waiting for a reply, Alexander turned, strolling from the room.

"Don't leave her! You have to stop the bleeding!" Simon shouted the words, but they were useless. "Rebecca. Bec. Open your eyes. Please. Cover the cut. It's too deep."

She said nothing as the lights went dim. Besides her slow heartbeat, the steady *drip, drip, drip* of her blood was the only sound.

CHAPTER 9

Simon

Simon felt it a few moments before it happened. He screamed for Alice—or anyone—to hear before he was gone for the day, leaving Rebecca to whatever fate awaited her.

When he landed beside the river in the in-between, he fell to his knees, dropping his head into his hands. She would die alone in her father's laboratory, and he was powerless to stop it.

A soft child's voice whispered beside him. "Get up. They'll find you if you stay by the river."

"I don't care."

A small hand wrapped around his, tugging him to get up. "Come on, Simon. You will help her when you get back, but you can't get back if they find you and send you to the other place."

He lifted his head, meeting Elizabeth's stare. Her eyes were bright, something like fear in them. She was worried for him. And she was right to be. She had found him that first day after he died and showed him where people like them went to hide. If the soldiers guarding this place found them, they would be sent to Hell, or so they assumed. Punishment for not dying properly, if that was how it went in the afterlife.

And now that he had a clear head, he knew Alexander wouldn't let Rebecca die. Not when she was the only leverage he had over Simon. When Simon was back, he would help her escape and let Alexander do whatever he wished to him.

But he could only help her if he wasn't captured by the soldiers who guarded the in-between.

Sighing, he let the child pull him up and followed her to their place beside the cave. She took up her usual spot, finding a stick to draw with.

Simon's mind raced as he worked through viable plans.

Everything circled back to one thing. He couldn't kill Alexander. The only way to ensure Rebecca and Sarah were safe would be to get them as far from the estate as possible. To do that, they would need money.

"Simon."

He looked up at Elizabeth standing over him, holding out a stick. "Not today, Elizabeth. I have a lot on my mind."

She pursed her lips, looking put out. After a moment, she said, "Can I help?"

Simon gave her a sad smile. "I wish you could, but these are adult problems. Not ones that can be solved by a child."

Elizabeth stuck out her lower lip and tossed the stick she had held out to him on the ground. "Adults always say that. I'm smart, you know."

Simon picked up the stick, dusting a bit of the gray dirt off before saying, "Very well, what game shall it be today? We can puzzle over this dilemma together while we play."

Elizabeth's mouth stretched into a wide smile as she picked up her stick and sat across from him. "Tic-tac-toe!"

"Of course, I should have guessed."

As they sat, scratching Xs and Os into the dirt, he continued to think. He had very few options, fewer still that would yield fruitful outcomes. When Elizabeth asked what his problem was, he explained he needed to find a job at night, but one that only required occasional assistance.

"Play the stock market," she said, as if that was the natural solution.

He pondered the idea, though, and the more he thought of it, the more weight it held. If he could secure a few hundred dollars, he could find a solid investment and turn it around. But where would he find that kind of money?

He asked the question aloud.

"Ask your Pa."

The answer sent a wave of pain crashing into him. His Pa, who now thought him dead was finding his own peace. How different things would be if only Simon had listened to him and not enlisted in the army? He could have stayed to run the paper, married Rebecca, and saved her from her father's machinations. Instead, he had died at the hands of Alexander and was forced to serve him for eternity.

"If only I could," he said on an exhale. "My pa believes me dead."

Elizabeth nodded. She understood these things far too well. She had died long before Simon. He knew that much, but talking of death with a child left him feeling unsettled, so they kept their topics light most days. She had been his only companion in the in-between, and as far as he knew, they were the only two who had evaded death.

When the day faded and his return to Earth was imminent, he steeled himself for what he would find.

Gasping as he sat up, he glanced around the dark room, taking in floral wallpaper decorating a small space, making it feel even more cramped. He ripped back the thin blanket and moved with preternatural speed up the stairs, stopping at the door to Rebecca's room.

Her steady heartbeat was a balm to his soul as he reached the side of her bed and breathed a deep sigh, watching her chest rise and fall under the blankets.

Sarah sat up in her crib, raising her arms. He glanced down at Rebecca and then at Sarah, who looked at him expectantly. Her piercing eyes were twins to Rebecca's father's, and something in her stare made him shiver.

"Rebecca," he whispered.

"Pick me," Sarah said into the silent space, thrusting her arms out more force-fully.

"Shhhh, you'll wake your mama."

"Pick me!" she said louder, her voice bordering on hysterical. Simon moved around the bed, pulling the small girl into his arms, and the sheen of wetness in her eyes cleared as she nestled into him.

"Are you hungry?" he asked, staring down at her perfect cherub face. She nodded. "Let's get you something to eat. Can I check on your mama first?"

She nodded again, and he leaned down, shuffling Sarah into one arm as he rested two fingers gently against Rebecca's throat. Her skin was warm and alive, and her heartbeat was strong. She was only sleeping; she would need her rest to recover from so much blood loss.

Taking Sarah down to the kitchen, he sat her in a chair before the long butcher block counter and opened the refrigerator. He found several prepared dish-es—waiting for the cook—and several dozen eggs.

He closed the refrigerator and went to the pantry, pulling out a jar of peaches and a jar of preserved apples from the shelf. Tipping his head outside the pantry, he held them both out. The pain in his wrists burned, but he swallowed the discomfort, painting a smile across his face.

Sarah squealed with delight, and he wondered if these weren't appropriate late-night snacks for a child. Still, he wasn't sure who had cared for her while Rebecca slept.

As he spooned heaps of preserved fruit onto a plate and handed Sarah a fork, he became even more concerned as she bit ferociously into the fruit, tearing at each piece like a wild beast.

"Maybe I should cut those for you," he suggested, but the ferocious look she gave him had him backing away.

When her plate was clean and she had licked her fingers, he brought her a cup of water and watched her gulp it down. The poor thing was ravenous. Setting her plate in the sink, he returned with a wet cloth and wiped her sticky cheeks and fingers.

Turning over her wrist to wipe the mess from her palms, he hovered over a birthmark shaped like a star. It was an exact match of the birthmark Rebecca bore in the same spot on her wrist. He ran a thumb over it, marveling at its likeness.

The hairs on the back of his neck rose, and he scooped Sarah up, darting for the door. He wasn't fast enough, though, and Astaroth appeared in the doorway, blocking his exit. He bared his teeth at the demon, tucking Sarah into the corner of his arm to shield her from the creature.

"Sssimon. I wonder what Alesssander would think of you caring for a child."

"You've done enough damage, demon. I was only feeding her a snack. I'll be down to see Alexander shortly."

"Sssee that you are." Astaroth didn't wait for Simon's reply, disappearing and leaving his path clear.

Simon raced up the stairs, finding Rebecca still asleep, and placed Sarah into the crib beside her bed. He pulled the soft yellow blanket up, tucked her in, and set her stuffed cat beside her.

When her eyes drifted closed, Simon left the room, going down to meet Alexander and whatever awaited him tonight.

CHAPTER 10

Rebecca

Rebecca's lids were heavy, and her skull felt as though it might split in two. She had woken only long enough to drink tea and warm broth and provide instructions to the house manager, Alice, on proper care of Sarah before falling into a deep sleep.

She knew it had been days, and somewhere, under the haze of drugs and her own body's weakness, terror for Sarah shot through her.

Her father had never taken so much blood before. Never drained her to the point of unconsciousness. And while some part of her hoped it meant he would not need more for some time, another part of her feared he would be draining Sarah of her life while she was too weak to protect her.

When she tried to lift her lids a second time, they came open, sticky at the edges, and she rubbed at them. It was late afternoon, and deep orange streaked the sky, threatening violence in the coming days.

"Mama."

The sweet sound of Sarah's voice made her chest ache, and she turned her head to find Sarah standing in her crib, staring over the lip. She reached her tiny hands out for Rebecca, silently asking to snuggle.

Rebecca propped herself on one elbow, feeling the lingering effects of whatever drugs her father had administered, and took a few steadying breaths before she sat up. She reached for the child, pulling her into the crook of her arm, and let her nestle in beside her, breathing in her sweet scent.

Sarah lifted one hand, casting the room in iridescent light as a kaleidoscope of butterflies danced overhead. Fear ran icy tendrils down Rebecca's spine as she wrapped her hand over Sarah's.

"No. Baby, you can't use your magic."

Sarah sniffled, a tear threatening to break free from her lashes.

"Oh, sweet girl, I'm not mad at you. I only want to keep you safe. You can never show your magic to anyone. Will you promise your mama?"

Sarah's watery eyes blinked several times, and a fat tear slid down her cheek, but she nodded. Rebecca wasn't entirely certain she understood, but she would remind her every day until she did.

"Are you hungry, sweet girl?" Sarah nodded once more, and Rebecca slid her legs over the side of the bed, needles pricking the bottoms of her feet. "Stay here. I'll get us something to eat, okay?"

She scooted forward, pressing her palms into the firm mattress, standing on shaky legs. The room spun precariously, but she took several steadying breaths before stepping forward. Pain shot up her calf and she collapsed to the floor, rubbing her spasming leg.

"Damn," she seethed.

It was fully dark, and she could just make out the light filtering up from several floors below. Gritting her teeth, she pushed off the ground, stamping her foot to ease the pain.

Warmth enveloped her as strong arms came around her and breath tickled her ear.

"I've got you."

Rebecca's heart thrummed in her chest as electricity sparked everywhere he touched her, and feelings of deep longing mingled with guilt flooded her.

She gasped, pulling out of his touch. "What's happening?"

Simon leaned with her, wrapping an arm around her waist. "You're weak and tired, but you need to eat. Let me help you."

"Would you get Sarah?"

At her words, he released her, lifting Sarah from her crib and spinning her in a circle before cradling her in one arm. Then he was back at Rebecca's side, wrapping his free arm around her waist.

She let him lead her, taking the stairs slowly, until they stopped beside a chair in the kitchen and she sat. Those feelings of longing and guilt evaporated, her mind clearing once more.

She looked up, meeting his amber eyes. "Simon, I'm so sorry. I had no idea my father was…" The words died on her lips as he handed Sarah to her and she settled the child on her lap.

Simon brought a plate and silverware to the table, setting them down in front of them and sliding into the chair beside her. "You need to eat."

She nodded, cutting bits of chicken into tiny slices, and fed them to Sarah, who gobbled everything hungrily.

Simon watched as they cleaned their plate, leaving only crumbs behind. "Motherhood suits you."

She looked up. "It's all I ever wanted for myself." Sarah grinned at them both, licking her lips. "Are you full, sweet girl?"

Sarah nodded and yawned loudly, leaning into her mother.

"Simon," Rebecca said.

He jumped up from his chair, holding his hands out for Sarah. She reached for him and squealed gleefully as he lifted her into the air and spun her.

"Simon, look at me."

"Let me take Sarah back to her crib."

38

Before she could say more, he was gone. Her chest rose and fell as images of Simon, chained to the ceiling, flashed in her mind. Hairs on the back of her neck prickled, and she knew he was behind her without looking.

She held her breath, waiting for him to say something, announce his return, and acknowledge her earlier words, but he said nothing.

She spun to face him. "Simon, please." The desperation in her voice cracked over the words.

Faster than her senses could comprehend, he was by her side, dropping to his knees. "Rebecca, I've tried to stay away. Tried to keep you safe, but..." His words died as his gaze trailed to her bandaged arm. "I failed you."

His throat worked to swallow some other unsaid words as his gaze met hers, pleading eyes searching her face.

Rebecca laid a hand on his cheek and stared back, willing him to see her, to understand. "Simon." She sucked in a breath. "I love you."

Simon searched her face for one more moment before he leaned in, letting his lips caress hers. The kiss was gentle and sweet, unlike their other kisses, which had been so full of passion. But in this moment, somehow, it was what she needed, and her heart melted as he ran one hand over her cheek. Feelings of adoration and devotion exploded through her.

When they broke their kiss, he leaned back but didn't release her. She stared into his eyes and knew she'd never felt love until this moment. She would give anything to see him smile at her like that for the rest of his life.

Rebecca shook her head, something in her brain finding fallacy in the last thought.

Simon's hand fell away from her cheek, and her mind cleared. Simon wasn't smiling, and those weren't her feelings. She looked down at his hand resting by his side.

"Simon."

"Yes," he whispered back.

She reached for his hand, placing it against her cheek again. Blinding admiration assaulted her, making her chest warm. She would spend her life proving she was worthy of him.

With some effort, she tore his hand away and sucked in a breath. "I knew it."

Some of the burning desire in Simon's gaze dimmed. "Knew what?" he asked, almost reluctantly.

"You have magic."

Simon sputtered a laugh, standing and pacing away from her. "What do you mean, magic? Like your father?" He turned back, expression hard.

"My father is not the only one with magic."

Simon's gaze turned wary. "What do you mean?"

"My entire family has magic."

"No. No, Rebecca. Magic is evil. Please tell me you haven't been using magic." He dropped into the seat beside her.

Their eyes met. "Magic isn't evil. My father is." She watched him as he processed her words, coming to some decision.

"I'm evil too, then. I've done terrible things for him."

"I never should have believed my father," she said, resting a hand over his fingers, nervously drumming on the table.

"I should have told you myself," he said after a long pause. "I was afraid."

"Afraid of my father?"

"Afraid of what you would think of me."

Rebecca swallowed again, remembering the night she had seen him in the orchard, dragging two boys back to her father.

"He made you do those things. I... understand. He would have hurt you."

Simon closed his eyes, pulling his hand free. "He did."

Tears formed along the edges of Rebecca's lashes. She had seen enough evidence of that and could only imagine what he had done to Simon to make him comply.

"But that wasn't what I meant. I'll tell you everything tonight. When you know the truth, you may change your mind." Simon stood, giving her a soft smile. "I need to see your father. Meet me in the orchard in thirty minutes."

He left the kitchen, stopping in the doorway to glance back at her before disappearing.

Rebecca wiped the wetness from her cheeks and stood, wincing at the pull in the stitches under her bandage. She moved to the door and out into the expansive foyer of her family home.

Dark banisters met at the bottom of a four-story climb, taking her all the way to the top floor and her room. Once, the family had been spread out, her father living on the second floor and her oldest sister, Mary, choosing to live on the third floor, calling it her wing and declaring it off limits to the others.

That left the fourth floor to Rebecca and Margaret, who had cared for her more like a daughter than a sister. Until she left.

But several years ago—around the same time her father had the gargoyles commissioned—he demanded everyone move to the fourth floor. It was around that time strange things began happening.

A boy Margaret fancied turned up dead, followed by several more over the years. Then, random incidents of fire began popping up all around their town. Although Rebecca hadn't known it then, her family was responsible for all of it.

She reached the top of the stairs and stopped to catch her breath.

She stepped into her room and her lips lifted in a smile. Sarah's soft snores came from the crib beside the bed as she leaned in, pressed a kiss to her forehead, and whispered, "I'll be back soon, sweet girl."

CHAPTER 11

Simon

Simon paced beneath the large oak tree where Rebecca often brought Sarah to sit. He had watched them so many times, never brave enough to approach.

Now, he would lay it all out for her and pray she accepted him. Fear spiked through him. He had already lost everyone. If he was forced to spend eternity under the same roof with her, knowing without a doubt she despised the thing he was, it would be torture.

A thousand times worse than anything he had endured at her father's hand.

The back door creaked open, and her favorite rose water perfume wafted toward him on a phantom breeze.

Simon stopped pacing, stuffing his hands into his pockets. He froze as she came around the corner and he took in the sight of her. Her lips were deep red, a stark contrast against too-pale skin; her bright, sparkling sapphire eyes met his as she stumbled, losing her footing.

He was by her side, catching her before she fell, and she clung to his arm, looking up into his eyes.

"Another of your magical abilities?" she asked breathlessly.

He hadn't considered any of his new gifts magic, but perhaps that was exactly what they were. More proof he was something vile, like her father.

Steadying her, he moved at her pace, stepping carefully over tree roots until they reached the base of the tree.

Rebecca slid to the ground, resting her back against it, and Simon followed, sitting beside her.

"Are you feeling a little better?" he asked, resting his shoulder against hers.

Her sigh was long. "Each day, I am a little closer to death."

Simon lifted his arm, wrapping it around her shoulder. "What can I do?"

She let her head rest in the crook of his arm. "My only fear is for Sarah. I never want Father to lay a finger on her."

Simon squeezed her gently. "I promise to do everything I can for her. And you."

Rebecca lifted her head, pulling out of his grip, and faced him. "It's too late for me. I only care about keeping Sarah safe now."

Simon's fingers trembled, and he curled his hands into fists at his side, taking a deep breath. "I want to be honest with you. And... no matter how you feel about me after, please know I will look after her."

Rebecca's gaze trailed to his shaking fists, and he willed them to be still. "Tell me," she whispered.

He opened his mouth. "I..." He'd imagined this so many times, but the words didn't want to come. He tried again. "I am bound to your father by magic."

Rebecca nodded as though she had already expected this.

"But..." He dug his nails into the palms of his hands, feeling the indentations in his skin, and relaxed his grip. "It's more than that. I bring demons back for him. So he may extract their essence to prolong his life."

Rebecca's lips turned down, but she gave him another encouraging nod.

"Before... me, he only extracted demons from humans who were possessed by them. Their bodies were inhabited." He took a shaky breath. "When they were extracted, the human died."

He closed his eyes, terror at seeing whatever expression was on her face, forcing them shut.

"Those boys," Rebecca breathed. "My father would have killed them?"

He nodded. "But I was stopping him. I wasn't bringing the boys to him."

Rebecca's hand flew to her mouth. "You weren't?" Her eyes sparkled in the moonlight, tears threatening to spill down her cheeks.

He should tell her all the times he brought humans to her father. He should tell her he had tasted human blood and liked it, even if he was working to keep those cravings in check, but fear was a living thing, and it strangled him. That was hope in her eyes. Hope that he wasn't the monster she thought he was.

"There's something else," he said, forcing the words past his lips before he lost his nerve. "I'm not alive."

CHAPTER 12

Simon

Rebecca flinched back as though she had been struck. "What?"

Simon's fingers were trembling again. Somehow, he had known this would be the thing she couldn't forgive. Could he blame her?

"Your father's experiment didn't just bind me; it ended my life."

Her gaze roved over him, looking for proof or perhaps something to discredit him. Her eyes lingered on his jacket sleeves, and she reached down, sliding them back and gasping. "Simon."

His gaze followed hers to the dark marks wrapped around his wrists, a brand forever reminding him of all the times he had been strung up in her father's laboratory.

She reached for his hands, and they trembled more violently as she placed hers over them and gave a gentle squeeze. She looked up, meeting his eyes again. For a moment, he thought she could see him as he truly was, but the moment passed, and she gave him a weak smile.

"I see only my dearest friend in the entire world. Nothing more and nothing less."

Simon let out a breath he hadn't known he was holding, some of the tension bleeding from his limbs, and squeezed her hands. They sat like that, staring at one another, hands clasped, and hope blossomed in his chest.

"What a tender moment."

The voice cut like a knife, scraping at Simon's insides. He released Rebecca's hands, getting to his feet and between Rebecca and the man he had never been able to protect her from.

Alexander chuckled, the sound like nails on a chalkboard. "You should be gone by now, Simon. Do you need encouragement to complete my tasks these days?" Simon squared his shoulders as Alexander approached. "Simon, move out of my way."

At his command, Simon's legs bent of their own accord, marching him to the left even as he fought the order.

"Rebecca, the babe is howling for you. Get inside and deal with it. I can't do any work with all that noise."

Rebecca jumped to her feet, racing past her father. She spared a look at Simon, mouthing, "I'm sorry," before she jogged toward the house.

When she was gone, Alexander faced him. "I thought I made it clear there would be consequences for your disobedience?"

Simon said nothing, his stiff legs rooting him to the spot.

"I have appealed to your soft nature, threatened you with her life, but nothing seems to work. If you want to spend time with my daughter, you will do so on your own time. To ensure fetching demons is your top priority, from now on, you have until one o'clock each night to bring me a body. Be it human or otherwise.

"If you fail to return within my set time, I will take what I need from Rebecca."

"You're killing her already. Why would I help you grow stronger?"

Alexander's eyes lit with amusement. "I see." He gave Simon a once over. "She'll die anyway. The doctors say it won't be long now."

Simon pulled uselessly against Alexander's restraint.

"Very well. A new deal, then. I won't touch her as long as you follow my orders to the letter."

Simon didn't believe him—not even for a moment, but he would be forced to do Alexander's bidding regardless of any deals they made. If this bought her time to recover and for him to form a plan, he would play along.

"The demon population wanes. Give me leave to travel farther, and I will devise a plan to bring back more at once."

Alexander rubbed his chin thoughtfully. "You will have until dawn, but if you bring back less than two demons, our deal is broken."

Simon nodded once, praying he hadn't made a fool's bargain.

"Go then. Bring me back at least two demons each night. If you fail, you know the consequences."

The spell released him, and he ran, not looking back, not pausing for even a moment.

The night had gone so much better than he could have hoped. In one evening, his faith that Rebecca might accept a creature like him was restored, and his bargain would give her a little more time.

CHAPTER 13

Rebecca

Rebecca stretched her arms overhead, relieved that the tug from her stitches was gone. The doctor had come after explicit instructions from her father to lie, saying she'd fallen in the woods and cut her arm on a branch.

When the doctor had inspected the perfect incision, she could tell he hadn't bought her story, but he said nothing, telling her he would return in two weeks to see if they were ready to come out.

To his surprise, the wound had healed remarkably quickly. When he tugged out the stitches, they marveled together at the thin white line where an angry red wound had been.

"You have some immune system, young lady," the doctor had said, scratching his head as he snapped his bag closed. "If only that immune system would fight this illness sapping your strength."

"I've been feeling much better," Rebecca said.

In fact, she did feel better. Not recovered, but not as weak as she once was. Since the night her father had taken so much blood, he hadn't called her back down to the dark room below their home, and it was doing wonders for her health.

On nights like tonight, when she could move about the room with ease, a trickle of hope seeped in. Doing her best to tamp it down, she crossed the room, humming as she folded her multicolored throw and laid it at the bed's end.

Sarah stood up in her crib, holding out her hands.

"Out."

Rebecca reached over the edge of Sarah's crib, lifting her out. Sarah was growing quickly, and Rebecca half expected her to be a grown woman the next time she checked.

"Do you want to see the flowers, my sweet?"

"Butterflies," Sarah said dreamily, making Rebecca smile.

"A wonderful idea!"

Sarah wriggled in Rebecca's arms and she set her down, laughing as the girl moved to the closet to find her shoes.

"We will need to move your clothes to your room soon. My closet is bursting with all your things," she teased.

Sarah threw the closet door open to inspect all her fine things. She would never thank her father even if he did support them, but she feared his growing generosity spoke of some new expectation he would level on them soon.

Rebecca pulled a light coat from its hanger and grabbed a jacket for Sarah. It was not yet fall, but the evenings were growing cool, and she wanted to soak up the fresh air for as long as possible before she was forced to return to the bedroom she would one day be permanently confined to.

Hand in hand, they strolled through the orchard, stopping at the fence. Sarah tipped her head back, staring all the way up the fence and at the gargoyles perched atop it before falling onto her bottom and giggling.

She spread her hands wide and blinked large blue eyes at her mother.

"Go ahead, you're safe out here." Sarah's small cheeks ballooned as she grinned widely, and butterflies erupted from her palms. They danced overhead, flitting between tree branches, and Rebecca watched as one landed on a leaf.

"That's very good, Sarah. Can you make anything else?"

Sarah wrinkled her nose, cupping her hands together; she bit her lip and squeezed. When she opened them, a tiny bug emerged, flying into the air.

"That's interesting," Rebecca said as the insect buzzed over their heads. It was on the tip of her tongue to ask what sort of bug it was when a soft yellow light flashed between its wings. "Is it a firefly?"

Sarah nodded enthusiastically, and Rebecca picked her up, swinging her in a circle. "Brilliant!"

They laughed together as Sarah made dozens more, releasing them into the air. Like her newest butterflies, they didn't burst when they touched other objects, and Rebecca wondered what else a person with that sort of magic might be capable of.

The afternoon stretched into twilight as Sarah ran between trees with Rebecca chasing after her, giving her kisses every time she caught her.

Alice brought their yellow blanket with two bowls of stew and they ate under the stars, wrapping their coats tightly around themselves.

"Your fireflies would be pretty at night, don't you think?" Rebecca asked as Sarah yawned loudly.

"Your turn, Mama," she said, yawning again.

Rebecca bit her lip. She'd never tried illusory magic before. She cupped her hands. "Like this?"

Sarah nodded.

"And I just imagine what I want to appear?"

Sarah wrapped her hands over Rebecca's.

"Fireflies," she whispered, and Rebecca said it with her.

She opened her hands and dozens of tiny bugs darted into the sky, blinking as they lit up the night. She leaned back, staring in wonder.

"Beautiful," a voice said, startling her.

"Simon!" Sarah squealed, running for him.

He caught her, scooping her up and kissing her cheek. "I brought you a present," he said to Sarah, and she beamed. "Hold out your hands and close your eyes."

She did, and he placed a small object in her palm. Opening her eyes, she beamed at him and wriggled to be free. He set her down, and she ran to Rebecca, holding out a plastic bottle.

"What is it?" Rebecca asked, taking the proffered bottle.

"Bubbles."

"Bubbles?" she asked, raising an eyebrow.

"It's new! A children's toy. Here, let me show you." Simon bent down, unscrewed the plastic cap, pulled out a small stick, and dipped it into the bottle. He blew, and bubbles erupted from the stick, floating lazily around them.

Sarah clapped her hands and snatched the bottle from Simon, dipping the stick in the bottle. She blew several times, water dripping off the stick, but no bubble came. She frowned and tried again.

Simon sat beside Rebecca, bumping her shoulder. She leaned into him as Sarah gave up on the bubbles and began creating her own. They both laughed as the girl set the bottle on the ground and danced away from them, chasing her creations.

"Don't you need to leave?" Rebecca asked.

"I have the night off for good behavior."

Rebecca glanced at Simon. "My father never takes a night off."

"He has company. I've been instructed to keep the *child* busy." He said "child" in her father's clipped tone, making her laugh.

"His loss is our gain." She tucked her arm into Simon's and pulled him up. "Come on, you can help me catch fireflies. I want to test a theory."

CHAPTER 14

Simon

Simon thought his cheeks might hurt forever. He couldn't imagine a time when he'd ever been happier. Rebecca and Sarah chased fireflies through the night, failing to trap the little buggers.

One would imagine creatures of their own making would be more compliant, but the insects buzzed higher and higher, narrowly escaping their captors at every turn. Eventually, he took pity on the girls and snatched the jar from Rebecca's hands.

He moved quickly, too fast for tiny imaginary insects, and captured four in one go. He screwed the lid on tight and handed his catch back to Rebecca. His gallantry earned him a kiss on the cheek, and he cast a glance over his shoulder at Sarah, who had settled herself onto the blanket and was nodding off.

"Let's put her in bed," he suggested.

Rebecca's smile faltered. "I don't know if I want her in the house with father's guest."

"I'll watch over her. You must be tired, too."

She didn't seem tired, though. She seemed more alive than he had seen her in weeks. His suspicion that her father's experiments were the reason for her poor health only grew. He had wanted to do none of the things her father asked, but on nights when two demons were impossible to catch, he did the only thing he could. He brought back humans.

Guilt tore at him, and he knew she would never agree to it if she knew her life came at such a cost, but he would choose her life over theirs for as long as she drew breath.

He scooped up Sarah, wrapping her in his coat and carried her inside. Rebecca trailed behind, holding her fireflies.

They moved silently, her father's dark laugh echoing down the hall, spurring them on. When they reached the bottom of the stairs, Simon looked back. "Stay here. I'll be back for you in a moment."

He disappeared, returning before she had time to protest, and lifted her into his arms, racing up the stairs in a blur of movement.

He set her gently on the bed and backed up.

"Wait... Don't go."

He stopped, frozen in the middle of the room. Her racing heart and the scent of arousal left him in no doubt of her intentions. He glanced at Sarah, breathing deeply in her crib beside them.

They had kissed a few times since renewing their friendship, but it hadn't gone further than that. He took a step toward her. Stopped.

She blinked up at him in the dark, a question in her eyes. He was frozen with indecision. Every fiber of his being begged him to go to her, to touch her, but if they crossed that line, there would be no going back for him. He would be destroyed. She would own him, body and soul—if he still had one.

Rebecca held out her hand. "Come here." Her voice was low, something feral in it.

53

He moved; his body reacted before he could stop it, and he was hovering above her. Her eyes were wide, a moment of shock playing across her face before she recovered herself, but it was enough to jar him back to his senses.

He dropped onto the bed beside her, leaning on an elbow. His arousal strained against his pants.

Rebecca's pulse thrummed at that delicate place where her throat met her collarbone, and it called to him.

He swallowed. "You must be tired."

"Not in the slightest," she said. Damn if her pheromones wouldn't be the death of him.

"Rebecca, I don't think..."

His words were cut off as she lunged for him, pressing her mouth to his and wrapping her fingers in his hair. He groaned as she slid closer, feeling how much he wanted her. She pressed her body more firmly against his as she sucked his bottom lip into her mouth and bit.

"Ow," he said around her teeth.

She released him, blinking. "I'm sorry," she whispered. "I'm sorry."

Her breathless words came between soft kisses as she trailed them over his lip to his ear, where she sucked again.

Giving in, he wrapped both arms around her, pulled her onto his lap, and groaned again as she rocked her hips, sending fire racing through his veins. Her lips reached the collar of his shirt and stopped as she worked the buttons on his shirt free, one by one.

When his chest was exposed, she ran a hand over smooth skin, letting her nail make light trails over his stomach.

"Remember, I don't heal," he gasped as her hand dipped below the waistline of his pants and found what she'd been seeking.

Her grip loosened a fraction, but her mouth was trailing toward her hand, and she was pumping her fist up and down his shaft with such enthusiasm stars were swimming at the edge of his vision.

"Rebecca," he breathed. She found the button of his pants, tearing it free with her teeth, and cool air brushed over the tip of him. Quickly, warmth replaced it as her mouth closed over its head and she sucked.

"Rebecca." He wrapped his fingers in her hair, intending to pull her mouth free, to give her some of the pleasure she was giving him, but her tongue flicked over the sensitive skin beneath the head of his cock, and his body convulsed.

He fisted her hair tightly as release came.

When the waves of pleasure stopped, his fingers flexed, and he released her hair, sucking in air. "I'm sorry. I didn't mean.."

She sat up, wiping her mouth with the back of her sleeve. "I've always wanted to do that," she whispered, sliding down beside him. She drew lazy circles on his stomach as he lay, trying to regain his faculties.

"Was I any good?"

"Good,"—he choked—"I forgot my damn name."

Her fingers stilled. "Simon?"

"Yeah?"

"I love you."

Simon rolled onto his side, facing her. "Rebecca, there's never been anyone for me but you and there never will be."

He kissed her, his fingers finding the hem of her sweater, and he tugged it over her head. Pressing his mouth to her bare skin, he ran his lips along her collarbone, sensing her essence pulsing beneath pale skin.

Pressing her back, he rose onto his elbows and stared down at her, taking her in. "You are perfect." Her cheeks flushed. "Now it's my turn to try something new," he said, sliding down her body until he reached the waistband of her skirt.

Finding the buttons at her hip, he ran his fingers over creamy skin as he unbuttoned each one. She lifted for him, and he slid the fabric down, exploring her bare skin. He tossed the skirt onto the floor and returned to her, starting at her calf, kissing his way up the inside of her thigh.

She spread her legs wide, an open invitation—one he gladly accepted.

When her body had come alive under his touch and he'd had to cover her mouth to keep anyone from hearing them, he knew he would burn the memories of their lovemaking into his brain. When she was gone, he would carry these moments with him and cherish the time they had, no matter how fleeting.

Her eyes drifted closed and he lay beside her, watching the rise and fall of her chest as something in him began to mend. It would break him to let her go, but it was the only way she would be safe.

He glanced over at the jar of fireflies buzzing against the glass. Rebecca was just like those fireflies: a bright light trapped within invisible walls. But he would find a way to free her.

CHAPTER 15

Simon

1943

Sarah turned three, Rebecca turned twenty-three, and the world was at war. Men from every state had been called to join the effort, leaving America with a dwindling population and far less crime.

For Simon, that meant demons were harder and harder to find. Pulled by death and despair to the most horrific places, many had left the United States. Alexander's youthful glow faded and his violent outbursts were becoming the norm.

For a short time, there had been an understanding between Simon and Alexander. And although his soul grew sootier with each human death, Rebecca had never seemed healthier.

Simon leaned back on his elbows, watching Rebecca as she made puffy rain clouds and dazzled Sarah with glittering rainbows. Her gifts were truly magical, and it was extraordinary to watch, but a sense of unease that he couldn't shake had settled over him. It told him their fragile peace was about to be shattered.

"Do fireflies, Mama." Sarah scooped a forkful of cake into her mouth and stared up at the night sky as Rebecca set hundreds of flashing lights loose into the night. She leaned down, whispering in Sarah's ear.

He could hear, but he let them have their secrets even as something warmed in his chest. No matter what, Sarah would have these small nightlights as a reminder long after her mother was gone.

Rebecca leaned back against Simon's shoulder. "I've been practicing. Want to see something neat?"

He grinned. "Always."

She scrunched up her nose, and a tiny glowing bug landed on Simon's shoulder, followed by another, and another.

Sarah clapped her hands. "Do me!"

Rebecca's brows furrowed in concentration. A tiny bug landed on Sarah's nose, lighting up. She squealed in delight and tried to catch it, but the bug zipped away, and she ran after it.

"You're getting better at controlling them."

"I'm not sure what use this skill will ever be," she laughed, "but Sarah enjoys my little tricks."

"You're an amazing mother. She's lucky to have you."

A tremor ran through Rebecca and she sat up, biting her lip. "Something's coming. Something I might not survive. I've had these dreams. I don't know what they mean, but I get a sense it's some sort of premonition of my future. Or my lack of one."

"Nonsense." Simon reached for her hand. He lifted her fingers to his lips, kissing each one. "I'll keep you both safe."

Rebecca looked down, extracting her fingers from his hold. "You know you cannot stop my father."

He flinched. She hadn't meant it as chastisement, but the rebuff stung nonetheless. He'd been doing everything he could to keep her safe, but she was right. It wasn't enough. Selfishly, he'd been enjoying their time together and had put little effort toward a plan for her escape.

"I've set aside a bit of money, and I'm working to get more. When I have enough, you and Sarah can leave this place."

Rebecca looked up, meeting his eyes. "You'll come with us?"

He swallowed a lump rising in his throat. "Rebecca," he said, "you know I can't."

"I won't leave you to my father. To be tortured by him."

"He won't. As long as I do what he asks."

"And what if he asks you to find me? To bring me back. You won't be able to ignore his request."

Fear such as he'd never known shot through him. She was right. Alexander could order Simon to kill her, and he would be forced to do it.

Sarah raced to her mother, falling into her lap. "Let's play!" she said, looking up.

Rebecca grimaced. "Soon, sweet one. Give me a few minutes."

Sarah stuck out her bottom lip. "Now."

Simon sat up, straightening the sleeves of his shirt. "It's okay, I need to go."

Rebecca grabbed his hand, stopping him. "Simon, I can't leave without you."

He forced his mouth to turn up at the corners, knowing it was a poor imitation of a smile. Knowing Rebecca would see through it.

She searched his face, waiting for a reply. When he said nothing, she released his hand, letting him go.

As he darted down the stairs into Alexander's laboratory, a stone settled in his stomach. Rebecca wouldn't leave without him; he had seen the determination in her eyes.

He had to find a way to go with them.

He reached the bottom of the stairs and flung the metal door open.

Alexander glowered at him from his place in the center of the room. "I can't say why you're in a foul mood. I'm the one who's been disappointed as of late."

Simon stalked to the table and crossed his arms. "I need to go to Europe."

Alexander let his amulet fall, and the room dimmed. "A trip like that would take months."

"I've thought about it, and there's no better option. There are hundreds, if not thousands, of demons. Astaroth confirmed it. Let me go, and I will find a way to bring back a horde."

Alexander arched a brow, the expression so like Rebecca's; something twisted in Simon's gut.

"If you go, I'll be left with no demons for some time. Where will I find the energy I need to thrive?" Alexander rubbed his chin, looking thoughtful.

"If you touch Rebecca, our deal is off," Simon growled.

"You've grown mighty confident, Simon. Need I remind you who runs things?"

Simon balled his hands into fists, working to get his emotions in check. It would do Rebecca no good if he lost his temper now.

"I will find as many demons as I can over the next several evenings. If you work to reinforce your gargoyle wards, you can keep them down here until you need them. They should last if you ration them."

Alexander flipped his leather journal closed, tucking it under his arm. "Very well. If you bring me at least fifteen demons, or humans with demons inhabiting them, which would frankly be easier to store, you may go abroad."

Simon dipped his chin, turning to leave.

"Oh, and Simon?"

Simon stopped.

"You had better think of a way to explain your absence to Rebecca."

CHAPTER 16

Rebecca

Rebecca paced the kitchen, leaning into the hall to check the clock again. It was nearly five in the morning. She hadn't seen Simon in three nights. Three nights of waiting like a fool with no word. Each of the previous days, when she pushed against his door, it didn't budge.

She'd tried using her air magic to force it; she'd called Alice to bring the key, but even with the door unlocked, it was stuck tight. It was as if Simon had some magic of his own that he'd employed to bar his door.

The grandfather clock tolled five, and Rebecca let out a huff of frustration. He must have traveled somewhere too far to come back. But he would have told her. He would have said he'd be gone.

Wouldn't he?

She dropped into a chair and planted her chin in her palm. He had disappeared previously. But that was before they declared their love for one another. *It wasn't before we shared our bodies,* she reminded herself.

Standing, she pushed her chair back and stormed down the hall of the servants' quarters. Simon's door was ajar. So he *was* there and he was avoiding her. She ground her teeth and dropped onto his thin mattress. It whined under her weight, and something hard poked her thigh.

She shifted uncomfortably, and the mattress coil dug deeper. Did he sleep on this mattress every night? On the nights he didn't stay in her room, she corrected herself. No, he didn't sleep. He had said so. He merely stored his body on this bed each day until he could return to it.

It was an hour before the sun rose; she could wait.

Rebecca stood and began to pace the small space, wrapping her arms over her chest as she traced a repeated path on the floor. The room was claustrophobic, and the wallpaper was dreary.

Glancing around, she noted no art on the walls or personal effects of any kind. He had lived with them for over three years and it was no more his home than a stranger's. How did he stand the cramped space? She reminded herself again he only used the room for storage.

It wasn't a life he'd chosen for himself, though. He was trapped there, just as she was. The difference was that his imprisonment was because of her. He had offered her a way out, told her to go, and all the while, he had been trapped, too.

If she left, if she escaped her father, there would be nothing keeping him there. Alexander would no longer have leverage over him.

But perhaps there was a way for both of them to be free. She bit her lip. For Simon to be free, her father had to believe they had separated. But what would ever convince her father of their separation?

She sat at Simon's desk and pulled a blank piece of paper from the drawer. Lifting the pen, she wrote:

Simon,

I'm so sorry. I never meant for any of this to happen. I was selfish. I know that now. How can I begin to put into words the pain I feel at your loss? If I had known what Father would do, could do, I would have let you go. Your chance at eternal happiness was snuffed out, betrayed by the person you most cherished. I will carry this sorrow with me for as long as I live. I know these words will never reach you. I know no one can reach you now. You are lost to me, to us all, forever. I shall pray your soul somehow managed to escape this hell you've been entombed in—for how long, none of us know. I pray that your soul at least rests with our Heavenly Father and can no longer see what has become of your earthly body.

With love,

Rebecca

On a second sheet of paper, she wrote:

Simon,

Find me, no matter the hour. I have a plan.

CHAPTER 17

Simon

Simon reached the edge of the estate just before morning. The dim line of pre-dawn light crested the horizon as he slid through the door and dropped three men on the floor.

"Astaroth," he bellowed, racing past them for his room. The demon appeared in his doorway as he flung himself into bed. "Get them downstairs," he said, and his last thought was a prayer that Astaroth would do as he asked.

When Simon landed beside the river in the in-between, he searched the misty distance for Elizabeth. When none of the shapes listing left and right appeared to be sentient, he left the river and trudged over dry, cracked earth, stopping at the mouth of their cave.

He swore as he reached it and saw at once no one was there.

"Elizabeth," he called. "Elizabeth, I need to speak with you."

No one answered. Rather than risk the foggy abyss, he sat, hoping she would return soon. Time drifted in some unknown pattern as he waited for Elizabeth or the day to end.

When his senses shifted, taking in the surrounding room, he knew something was off. There had been no time to warp the wood before he slid into bed the night before, which meant his body had been defenseless all day.

Sulfur hung heavy in the air, and it wasn't Asataroth's.

He sat up, glancing around the space. Nothing was out of order. The pen atop his desk sat in its usual position, along with the three suits he owned, apart from the one he had hung from a peg in the corner.

He slid his legs over the edge of the bed and stood, listening. The house creaked, settling in for the night, and the sounds of the home's occupants blended into a soft melody as they went about their night's tasks.

He left his room, going down the hall to the back stairs, stepping lightly. The smell of sulfur grew stronger.

He was only two demons shy of his promise. He would capture the final two this night and tell Rebecca of his plan. While he was away, too far for Alexander to reach him, and with no time restraint holding him to the property, she could run. Take the money he'd saved and book passage with him across the ocean.

When they were far enough away, Alexander couldn't force him back.

Alexander always thought of everything, but he hadn't thought of placing a restriction on the amount of time Simon could go. As long as Simon stayed in Europe, he was out of Alexander's reach.

Alexander would send Astaroth to retrieve him. He was counting on it because Alexander had never explicitly forbidden Simon from draining the demon dry. And although demons could return, it would take him some time.

Simon would spend the rest of Rebecca's life draining him if that was what it meant to ensure she was safe. Finally, they would be free of him. He hadn't imagined this future, but now that it was in his grasp, he would do anything to have it.

As he pushed the door open, light flooding the dim space, his dreams shattered.

CHAPTER 18

Simon

Time moved in slow motion as Simon sped through the room, sinking his teeth into the first demon and wrenching it across the room. He reached for the second as it misted into nothing and slid down Rebecca's gaping mouth.

"Noooooo!" he screamed, reaching her as she dropped to the floor. He caught her, cradling her head in his arms. "Rebecca. Rebecca, open your eyes," he begged. "Please!"

He rocked her as terror shot through him.

She was still, her soul fighting the demon—and losing. He'd seen it a dozen times. Sometimes, they took only minutes; other times, it was hours. But eventually, the demon won, forcing the human's soul to depart the body.

He pressed his forehead to hers, a tear escaping his lashes to drip onto her smooth cheek. Her body convulsed, and he wrapped her in his arms, cocooning her in his embrace.

If he could only pull the demon from her before she lost the battle.

His canines lengthened and he bit into her neck, sucking deeply. Effervescent life-giving blood ran down his throat, and it was like nothing he had ever tasted.

It was the most intoxicating thing he had consumed. He sucked harder, pulling her life force into him.

It was sweet, like crisp apples and chocolate, mixing to form the most exquisite drink. Something about that registered in his mind: humans tainted by demon essence had a bitter tang, something almost rancid in their blood.

Rebecca's blood was pure. She wasn't possessed. Not yet. And he was sucking out her life. He pulled back, wrenching his lips from her tender flesh. "Rebecca, I'm sorry. Please, fight."

Alexander's low chuckle rebounded from the circular walls of his laboratory as he stepped into the room. "You'll kill her all on your own."

Simon glared up at him. "You did this," he demanded. "You set the demons free and sent her down here."

Alexander folded his arms over his chest. "I released the demons, yes. But Rebecca came down here all on her own. She was going to leave you. She told me so herself."

Simon shook his head. "She would never say such a thing. She loves me."

Alexander tossed a note at his feet.

"I told her what you've been doing to keep her safe. My daughter deserves better than a monster like you."

Simon reached for the note with one hand, even as he cradled Rebecca in the other. He tore it open, reading her words. He read them again. She was... condemning him? Blaming him? Calling him a soulless creature.

"What did you tell her?" He spat the words, panic gripping him. She would die, and her last thoughts of him were that he was a monster.

"I told her you've been bringing me humans. Not demons. And all of your own free will."

Simon glared up at him, meeting his steely gaze.

"Did you think you could fool me? I'm thrice your age and have seen more of the world than you ever will. Did you think you could devise a plan I wouldn't see through?"

Simon dropped the note, wrapping his arm around Rebecca as she seized in his arms, foam spewing from her lips. He squeezed her body, attempting to calm the shivers rolling over her. "Rebecca. Fight it. Fight the demon. You're strong."

Alexander tsked. "Even when she has abandoned you, cast you aside, you would stand by her?"

"You forced her to write this. You're sick. I would put nothing past you."

Alexander leaned down, retrieving the note even as his daughter shook and spasmed. "I'm tired of your chivalrous heroics. You promised me demons, and you will deliver. Simon, drop Rebecca."

Simon shouted in frustration as his body acted against his will, tossing her twitching body to the floor. "Rebecca. Rebecca, I love you. I'm sorry! Please fight."

"Simon, shut up." He groaned the command as if his cold, unfeeling heart cared nothing for the daughter dying at his feet.

Simon's pleas halted abruptly.

"Simon, stand."

He did, wishing any part of him could retaliate against the monster holding his strings.

"Now, Simon, listen to me. You will leave, get on the next ship and depart for England. When you reach our sister land, go where the demons converge. Do not return until you have collected one hundred demons. I don't care if they inhabit bodies or float on a breeze. You may not set one foot on this property until you have done what I ask of you."

The spells binding Simon in place remained taut. It was his only sign there would be more demands.

Alexander cleared his throat to deliver the rest of his speech.

Rebecca sputtered, bile dribbling over her lips.

Simon tried to pry his mouth open, tried to fall to his knees and hold her, but he stood, immobile, watching as she rolled to her side and coughed, blood leaking down her chin.

He screamed internally, begging whatever god listened to grant him this one moment to go to her, to comfort her.

She coughed again as dark smoke poured from her mouth, forming a solid shape above her. She fell back, motionless, and the demon's red eyes narrowed on Alexander. Simon watched Rebecca's chest rise and fall as elation shot through him.

She had won. Somehow, she had fought the demon and *won*.

He had only a moment to consider it before the demon struck, attacking Alexander with feral strength.

Alexander formed a shield of fire in front of him, sending the demon dancing back.

Simon could tell at once it was no low-level demon. The thing had presence of mind; its calculating red gaze searched the room for a counter strategy, intent on winning its prize. Alexander had long known his soul was of particular interest to the demon population—one as black as his was like a beacon.

It was half the reason he'd spent a small fortune on spells and gargoyles to ensure they couldn't reach him. As a further precaution, he had moved to the fourth floor, where no demon could tread.

Rebecca moaned softly, capturing Simon's attention.

It drew Alexander's, too, and something flashed in his eyes before he said, "Simon, protect me. End the demon and leave the estate. You have your orders."

Simon's body moved, and his mouth opened wide, sucking in the demon's essence. It gave him strength, but not enough to fight the spells binding him. When the demon disappeared, his feet moved, carrying him through the broken bars of the fence.

He stopped, inhaling sharply for the first time that night.

"Rebecca!" he shouted. "Rebecca, I'll be back!"

He stood on the other side of a fence he had hated for three years, wishing for the first time he was still trapped inside.

CHAPTER 19

Rebecca

Rebecca grunted, every part of her body aching. Even that small sound was like fire in her throat. She felt as though she had been burned from the inside out.

Cracking heavy lids, she squeezed one eye shut against the harsh mid-day sun streaming through her windows. "Hello," she croaked, not recognizing her own voice.

Something moved in her periphery, and she blinked, eyes watering. "Who's there?"

A form stood over her, blocking the light.

"Who... Who are you?" she breathed.

"Hush, child. You need rest. You have been through quite an ordeal."

A cool hand pressed against her cheek. She fought the encroaching darkness, peeling her eyes open. Light, blindingly bright, burst through the room. She squinted, trying to make sense of the scene. Not one, but two brilliant forms lit the room with their glow.

She tried again to open her eyes, but pain drummed against her skull. She let her lids fall closed, and voices drifted to her.

"We must do something. It should not have entered her body."

"She exorcised the demon. She will recover, Gabriel."

"Move aside."

"You bade me remind you she would be safer if you let her live out her mortal life."

The voices drifted away, and she was swallowed by darkness.

All was still and dark. Rebecca's first thought was for Sarah. Some internal clock told her she'd been asleep too long.

Her eyes flew open, and she sat up. The room spun wildly before it settled, and she blinked, staring into an empty crib.

"Sarah," she rasped. She stumbled out of bed, toppling to the floor, and crawled to the door. "Sarah." Her voice broke as tears slid down her cheeks. "Sarah!"

She sat against the door, tears falling freely. "Sarah, my sweet girl, where are you?"

A door across the hall flew open. A woman Rebecca had never seen rushed out, wrapping a robe tightly around herself. "Miss, you shouldn't be out of bed," she said, pulling Rebecca to her feet and turning her toward the door.

Rebecca wrenched her arm from the strange woman's grip. "No. I need to find Sarah."

"Sarah is just fine. She's sleeping in her room."

"*Her* room? No. Sarah sleeps with me."

The woman dipped her head, not meeting Rebecca's eyes. "Mr. Graves says she's old enough to sleep in her own room, miss."

Rebecca eyed the woman. She couldn't be more than eighteen and was dressed in nightclothes.

"Has my father hired you?"

"Yes, ma'am. To look after the girl. My name is Thea."

Rebecca bit back the words threatening to spill from her tongue. It was not this girl's fault her father had overstepped. She would not take her anger out on her.

"I'll see my daughter now," she said, moving past the woman.

She found Sarah in Elizabeth's old room. It was the room she'd planned to give Sarah when she was older, but she had never been able to part with her. Seeing her stretched out on a crib unused for more than two decades, with nothing but a blue blanket for company, something in her chest seized.

She rushed into the room, scooping her daughter into her arms, and squeezed her tight. Sarah wriggled in her arms, making small grunting noises as she tried to get free, but Rebecca ignored her, hugging her close as she returned to her room and settled Sarah on the bed beside her.

With Sarah nestled into her side, she closed her eyes and fell into a deep sleep.

Bombs crashed into the earth, detonating amidst unsuspecting people and bodies, and their parts were flung hundreds of yards in every direction.

The air was filled with screams and wails as each bomb took dozens of lives and injured countless others.

Rebecca walked among them, resting a gentle hand against the forehead of a pale-faced soldier no more than seventeen. His body shook with tremors, but he couldn't move his head enough to see his mangled body. It was better that way.

What was left of him couldn't be mended.

She knelt beside him and gripped his hand, whispering a prayer for his soul. "Am I gonna die?" he asked through clenched teeth.

She pressed a kiss to his cheek. In a voice that wasn't her own, she said, "Yes. But your soul will be in Heaven."

A single tear slid down his face as he blinked once before his eyes glazed, staring at nothing.

Rebecca was propelled backward, shooting through space and time to land on her bed.

She blinked, sucking in a breath, and touched her fingers to her cheeks, wiping away tears.

Glancing to her right, she found Sarah tucked into the crook of her arm and sighed. A dream. It was a dream. No doubt some manifestation of the horrid news that had been reported of the war these past six months.

Six months. The length of time since Simon had been wiped from her universe and her whole world had imploded. She hadn't believed her father at first, but when a week stretched into a month and one month turned into two, she knew it must be true. Simon wouldn't leave her again. Not willingly.

Her father had found a way to end him. Permanently.

Now, she had only one reason to go on: Sarah. She pulled the girl closer.

She had turned twenty-four a few weeks ago. Sarah was four. The pain was back. And the weakness. Somehow, none of it mattered.

Thea came into the room, sliding the curtains back. Rebecca rolled onto her side, away from the light.

"Come on, Rebecca, Sarah will want to play with you. Let's get dressed."

Rebecca pulled her blankets over her head. Sarah squirmed beside her, kicking at the covers.

"Mama, stop."

Rebecca groaned, but let the blankets fall away.

Sarah sat up, holding her hands out for Thea, who scooped her up and set her down beside the bed.

"Come on, Mama. It's pretty."

Rebecca rolled over, giving them her back.

"Let's go down and have some breakfast," Thea said.

"No." Sarah's stubborn tone meant she was brewing for a fight today.

"We should let your mama rest, Sarah."

"No."

The blankets were tugged off the bed, and Rebecca rolled over to meet her child's steely-eyed stare.

"Mama's tired, sweet girl."

"Get up," Sarah said.

Rebecca sighed. "If I come to the garden, will you be content?"

Sarah appeared to consider, then nodded.

Rebecca gave her a weak smile and slid her legs over the side of the bed. "Let me dress, and I'll be down in a moment."

Sarah gave her a wary look, deciding Rebecca's words were true, and left the room, dragging Thea behind her.

When Rebecca was alone, she swallowed back a sob and repeated the words she said to herself every day since Simon left them. "I will make it. I will be strong for Sarah."

When she could stand, she did, going to her closet and wrapping a shawl around her nightdress. If her father saw her dressed this way, he would chastise her, but he had already taken everything. What more could he do?

She slid soft slippers onto her feet and left the room, going slowly down the stairs. As she approached the first floor, Sarah's giggles carried in the foyer, warming some long-frozen part of her.

Stepping into the kitchen, she smiled.

Sarah and Thea froze, looking guilty.

"By all means, carry on," she said, dropping into a chair as Thea and Sarah resumed their game. Sarah flung a handful of flour at Thea, who dodged it, only to fling a fistful of sugar back.

They continued their dance, coating every surface in white.

"It's the best this kitchen has looked in years," Rebecca said, giving them another half smile.

Sarah slid to a stop beside her mother and wrapped white, powdered hands around her neck. "I'm glad you're back, Mama."

The words cleaved a hole in her chest. She had mourned Simon's loss, but it had been at the cost of Sarah's happiness. And for that, she felt a different kind of ache. Sarah deserved better.

Rebecca reached into the flour bowl and scooped out a handful, flinging it at Sarah, who dodged the blow. She laughed hysterically, reaching into the bowl and flinging powder into her mother's face.

Rebecca giggled, grabbing Sarah around the waist before she could escape and squeezing her into a hug. "I love you, sweet girl," she whispered into Sarah's ear, setting her down.

CHAPTER 20

Simon

Simon moved alongside a wall, waiting for the soldiers to march by. He was deep behind enemy lines, where the heaviest concentration of demons congregated. He would have assumed he'd found the camp by sheer luck if he wasn't confident Alexander's magic was at work.

There had been no way he could know where he was headed when he disembarked and followed an instinct to run in this direction.

Now, he'd been at this forsaken camp for close to nine months, and he was beginning to see the hopelessness of his mission. While there was no shortage of demons, he could not conceive of a way to bring one hundred of them on a boat back to Bath, North Carolina.

It hadn't needed to be plausible when it was only meant as his escape, but now it was the thing keeping him from Rebecca.

He had tried capturing as many at once as possible and hooking them on his fingers, but he could never move more than four, and the moment he reached a temporary destination and set his body down to rest, they escaped.

There was no scenario where he could capture them beyond dawn.

He kicked a rock, leaning into the wall. He'd thought himself so clever, and now he was destined to spend eternity camped out in whatever den of depravity drew the largest crowd.

As with most nights, his thoughts strayed to Rebecca. With no new demon essence to sustain him, had Alexander resorted to stealing from her again? Was she suffering? Would she die without him there to protect her from her father?

Several too-thin captives stumbled by, carrying buckets to their barracks. The first night Simon had arrived, he'd snuck into their rooms, expecting to have to fight off soldiers, but what he saw had him retching outside for an hour.

The humans inside were little more than skeletal remains, cheekbones cutting jagged lines across their faces. They stared with gaunt eyes when he entered, some not registering his presence.

He'd begun hunting for them, bringing back rats or squirrels, anything he could find to help them, but there were too many of them and not enough wild creatures to feed them. He pillaged Nazi food stores and ran as far as the magic would allow to search the countryside, but everyone was starving, and stealing from one mouth to feed another might mean choosing who starved that night.

He had never known life could be this bad. Suddenly, all his father's warnings rang true. He was a fool for ever thinking he knew anything about the world or human nature. If he had shipped off to war at eighteen, green behind the ears, the war would have chewed him up and spit him out.

Alexander paled in comparison to the creatures this war produced.

As he explored the camp each night, drawn to the places where demons dwelled, he was forced to observe new and terrible horrors.

The men who ran the camp delighted in experimenting on its captors. Some used technology to flay their victims; others found sick pleasure in extracting pain with their bare hands.

If he ever escaped this place, he would burn it to the ground on his way out.

When the camp quieted, soldiers heading to their tents or into town to find entertainment, he darted to the kitchens, pilfering the potatoes he had seen come in earlier in the night. They were meant to feed the soldiers, which was an easy choice for him. He filled two buckets to the brim and dashed into the prisoner's barracks.

They were healthier already, and several moved to collect the vegetables as he dumped them on the ground. "Cook them first. Don't let them poison themselves," Simon instructed. It wasn't something a grown man needed to hear, but these men were starved beyond rational thought. One man nodded, clapping him on the shoulder, and he dipped his chin.

Simon raced back to the kitchen with his buckets, refilling them, and dumped them out in the next tent. This tent was lighter each night, several of its residents having been shipped off to other places.

He had tried to follow, but the commands binding him forced him to remain here. He knew there were camps set up for those who were too ill to work, filled with the dying. But try as might, he couldn't go to them.

When he had delivered potatoes to all the prisoner's tents, he moved through the dark to the medical tent. There was only one, and it was used to treat only the soldiers.

Lifting the lid of a medical kit, he found a pain-sedating serum and several needles and grabbed them, taking them back to the third tent. A man approached, kissing the backs of his hands as he took the medicine. "Thank you," he said in broken English, and Simon's chest ached.

He wished there was more he could do for these poor souls.

He froze as sulfur filled the air. Just as he had expected, several demons filtered into the tent, hovering over the men. They didn't seem to notice as demons tested them, searching for pain and suffering.

These demons weren't looking for bodies to inhabit. They were here to feed on the weak and dying.

One of the demons noticed him and bared his dark teeth. It misted out of existence, leaving the others behind. Two more spied him and shrank into the shadows. Clearly, his reputation among the demons in this camp was spreading.

While he hadn't found a way to capture even a fraction of what he needed for her father, he had thinned their ranks, easing some suffering.

Two more demons spotted him and evaporated, leaving only one. He approached the dark form as it latched on to a dying man. It was too caught in the throes of his misery to see Simon coming. He let his teeth lengthen as he drove them into the creature and drained it in moments.

Wiping green from his lip, he wondered if this would be his new eternity.

CHAPTER 21

Rebecca

Rebecca woke from another dream, wiping her damp forehead on the back of her sleeve. This time, she had seen Simon. He was fighting against the Nazi soldiers, helping turn the tide of the war. She smiled at a dream that would never be his reality.

If Simon had lived and had never met Rebecca, that would have been his fate. He would return as a decorated war hero, and his father would be proud.

Instead, his loved ones had mourned him in a farce of a funeral years ago, and only Rebecca and her father knew the truth.

And Sarah.

She looked over and sat up. Sarah wasn't in bed beside her.

"Sarah! Sarah, where are you?"

She tried to keep the panic from her voice, but these days, every small thing set her on edge.

Sarah would be five in less than a month. She was old enough to look after herself, but Rebecca couldn't stop the fear that seized her whenever her daughter was out of sight.

Sarah bounded into the room, swinging the door wide to let in more light.

"Mama! Wake up! The war is won!" Sarah twirled a small American flag, dancing in a circle.

Rebecca rubbed her eyes, some of the panic easing her chest. "What do you mean, darling?"

"The Soviets have Berlin surrounded!"

Thea rushed in, grabbing Sarah's hand. "I'm sorry, Rebecca. We were listening to the news."

Rebecca shook her head. "It's no problem. Come here, Sarah. Give me a kiss."

Sarah pulled free from Thea's grasp and ran to Rebecca, kissing both her cheeks. "Love you, Mama.

"Love you too, sweet girl."

"Will you come outside?" Sarah danced away, waving her flag again.

Rebecca pressed a hand to her temple. "Not today, my love. Will you bring me something from the garden?"

Sarah nodded and skipped out of the room. Thea gave Rebecca a nervous nod and followed Sarah, closing the door.

When they had gone, Rebecca fell back on the bed, sighing. Although her father hadn't touched her in nearly a year, she felt her strength waning. Somehow, she knew time was running out.

Death frightened her, but she was more worried for Sarah. Sarah had powerful gifts, like Rebecca, and they would be difficult to hide. She had tried to explain to Thea how important it was to keep Sarah's gifts hidden from Alexander, but Thea had only nodded, eyes wide with terror, and left the room the moment the conversation ended.

If only Rebecca were a man. She could have made her own fortune; carved a path that didn't include Alexander. If only she hadn't relied on Simon to save them. But it was too late for wishing, and her greatest fear was that Sarah would be doomed to repeat her mistakes.

As she lay back, breathing deeply, her eyes fluttered closed, and she slipped into another dream of a land far from home.

CHAPTER 22

Simon

"You don't have a spade?"

"I played my last spade in the last round!"

"I know you have a four!" Simon demanded, throwing his cards down. "You're a cheat, Williams."

Simon stood, pushing the table back, and several of the men grumbled their agreement.

The man beside him, Williams, tossed his cards on the table. All red.

"Check under his waistline."

Two men at the table grabbed Williams by the wrists as one ran a hand along his waistband.

Williams blew the first man a kiss. "I got somethin' for ya," he said, winking at the other man.

"Carey was right!" the man said, holding up a four of spades. "He's a cheat!" Everyone at the table began hurling accusations, and several men scooped up bottle caps, rocks, and other objects used for betting. "Wadaya wanna do with 'im, Carey?"

Simon turned around to face the group of men. He paused, watching their expectant faces. If he condemned the man, they would call for blood. They were that loyal. "Let him go, guys," he said, slapping one of the men on the back. "We're all friends here. Just don't let Williams near your wives."

The men laughed, releasing Williams, and he stumbled away, leaving before they could change their minds.

It was a miracle what just a few months had done for them, and though he would never forget the men who no longer occupied the empty tents, this group of eighty or so thrived on the rations he brought them each night.

"Shhhh shhh shh," someone said, snuffing out their light as boots marched over gravel outside the tent.

Simon ducked against a wall, melting into the shadows. He stuffed a hand into his pocket, crumpling an envelope.

Pulling it out, he smoothed the corner, checking to ensure Rebecca's name and address were still legible. With no return address, he had no way of knowing if any of the letters he sent ever escaped this war-torn country and found their way to her, but continued to write them, hoping at least a few got through.

The tent flap flew open, and a dozen soldiers marched inside. They stood at attention as the man in front spoke.

"Aufmerksamkeit! Der Krieg ist vorbei! Sie werden nach hause zuruckehren." The man saluted the air and turned, marching out of the tent. The other followed, and Simon returned to the crowd.

"What did they say?"

Williams answered from across the tent. "The war is over. We're going home."

All around him, men cried out, sucking in gasping sobs. They hugged one another, eyes red, cheeks streaked with tears.

Simon was grabbed roughly around the waist and squeezed. Soon, the group encircled him. A cheer rose, and every man had hope in his eyes.

His chest buzzed with a warm sort of joy, but underneath it was unease. He had observed the soldiers and scientists in this camp for more than a year, and no part of him believed they would so easily let the men go.

He extracted himself from the group and slipped outside.

Simon scaled the back side of the tent, following the shadows until he reached the commander's tent. Something bumped his shoulder, making him spin around. Williams was beside him, pressing a finger to his lips.

"If you're thinking what I am, you'll need me to translate," he whispered. Simon nodded, tilting his head toward the door.

They moved silently, Williams putting Simon to shame for all his stealth. It was obvious the man hadn't been a run-of-the-mill soldier. They stopped under an air vent outside the commander's tent and listened.

The words were distorted, but Simon could make them out. He murmured in Williams' ear; the man went pale beside him. He motioned for them to go, and they stepped lightly, returning to the prisoners' tent.

Williams grabbed his arm just outside the flap. "Wait." Simon stopped. "They're going to take us to another camp. They'll march us there and let us die along the way. They'll never give us up."

Simon nodded. It was no less than he'd expected. "Then we escape tonight."

The other man bobbed his head in agreement, and they stepped inside the tent.

CHAPTER 23

Simon

Simon hated seeing the light dim from their eyes as he told the men the truth. They had survived unimaginable torture, only to be killed at the end of the war. It wouldn't come to that—not if he had anything to say about it.

He raised his hands, and a hush fell over the group. All eyes were on him, and he felt the weight of their hope.

"We'll make a break for it tonight. I've been watching their patrol routes for months." There were several nods and murmurs of agreement, but some of the men looked dubious, and he knew they would need more convincing. "We've got one shot. I can't promise we'll all survive this, but I know we won't if we put our trust in the Nazis. Will you take your chances with me? Or the soldiers?"

A cheer rose from the crowd, followed by another, and doubting faces turned to ones of conviction as backs straightened, some of their old resolve returning.

Simon nodded, and they crowded closer, everyone listening intently. "Here's the plan…"

When Simon had selected eight other men to lead groups of ten, they went on the same rotating schedule he'd drawn out for them in the sand. Six soldiers passed by their tent every forty-three minutes, and, directly after, sets of two marched by every four minutes. There was a nine-minute break between the last set and the first.

When Simon had cut through the barbed wire fence behind the cook's tent, making a space large enough for them to pass through, the men used the nine-minute break to steal through the camp and out into the night.

The cook was a liability they couldn't afford, but Simon felt no guilt taking the life of a man who regularly slipped poison into the prisoners' food on the scientists' orders.

Every three hours, the last set of soldiers checked inside the tent to ensure the prisoners had not escaped. While they had used objects around to stuff some of the beds, prisoners needed to be present—moving and breathing—to make it believable.

Simon was part of the last two groups to leave, bringing up the rear—the strongest and the fastest. It gave the first seven groups a three-hour head start on the soldiers.

His group and Willams' would need to outrun the dogs.

He shuffled under a thin blanket, groaning, and the other men did the same as two heads leaned into the tent. One of the soldiers said something to the other, and Simon tensed.

After a moment, the tent flap closed, and he sighed. Beside him, Williams tore back his sheet, and the others shot up.

"Nine minutes," Simon mouthed to the group.

Williams went first, followed by nine other men. Simon dipped his chin, and his group followed. When they reached the cook's tent, he stopped, looking back. In the distance, he could just see the group of six soldiers coming around a tent. He set his mental clock for forty-three minutes.

In forty-three minutes, the might of the Nazi army would begin the hunt for them.

Simon trailed behind his group, listening for the sounds of attack even as he carefully retraced the path he'd laid out for the prisoners. If even a single landmine buried around the camp was triggered, they would all be discovered.

It was another hour-and-a-half to the port of Barth and the most dangerous part of the journey.

When forty-three minutes had passed, just as he'd expected, a siren blared. It was close enough that the men in his group could hear it, and several of them gave up their cautious treading and ran outright.

"Careful!" Simon whispered loudly.

When they cleared the trees, he breathed a sigh of relief. One of the men, Brown, looked back, but he waved him on. Turning, Brown ran, not looking back again.

When the last of the men were out of hearing, Simon raced back to the camp. It was in chaos. Soldiers scrambled to pull on uniforms and form lines as dogs were leashed and dragged from their beds. Scraps of clothes and blankets were thrust into the dog's faces and a man at the front of the group shouted orders.

Simon slipped into the cook's tent, finding the gasoline he had stored there, and ripped the lid off.

Running along the camp's perimeter, he doused tents and ran a line of gasoline along the ground between them. It wasn't enough to destroy the camp, but it would slow them down, and perhaps it would delay the dogs.

Lighting a match, he dropped it, watching as flames ignited along the ground and tore a path toward the nearest soldier's tent. Shouts quickly turned to screams as the tent was swallowed in smoke.

Simon stayed to watch only long enough to see the sky darken with thick smoke before he darted into the forest and away from the horrors of the past twelve months.

CHAPTER 24

Rebecca

A soft breeze caressed her face, and Rebecca sighed, the warmth in her chest buzzing to life.

Soon, light. Those words had been a whisper in her mind, a thought that didn't belong to her. When her eyes fluttered open, harsh daylight made her skull pound.

"Thea," she called weakly.

Thea moved softly into the room. "Yes, Rebecca?"

"Could you please close the curtains?"

Thea nodded, crossed to the far wall, and pulled the sheer pink fabric closed, though it did little to dim the light filtering through. Rebecca squeezed her eyes shut, desperately wishing to return to her dream.

In it, she was surrounded by brilliant white, and everything glowed. In that place, she was filled with a peace and contentment she had never known. It was as though she were whole in a way she never had been.

Rebecca opened her eyes, letting her head roll to the side where she saw Sarah hugging the doorframe.

"Come here, sweet girl." Sarah looked to Thea for confirmation and something fiery flared to life in Rebecca. "Sarah, come to your mother."

The girl darted glances between Thea and Rebecca, her eyes welling with tears. Rebecca winced, lifting onto her elbows.

"I'm sorry, sweet girl."

Thea moved to the girl and scooped her up. "Come on, Sarah, let's give your mama a hug."

She brought Sarah to Rebecca's bed and set her gently beside her. "Why don't I leave you two and make some tea?" She left the room, not waiting for a reply.

The wetness was back in Sarah's eyes, pooling at the edge of her lashes. "I'm sorry. Mama didn't mean to frighten you. Have you been to the garden today?"

Sarah nodded and cupped her hands together. When she opened them, small iridescent butterflies burst from her hands and fluttered in the air.

"That's beautiful," Rebecca said, wrapping her arm around Sarah's waist and tugging her closer.

Sarah leaned into her, her weight pressing into Rebecca's chest. She sucked in a breath, and Sarah sat up.

"Sorry, Mama." Her lower lip trembled, and a tear spilled down her cheek.

"Sarah, I know you're scared, but please don't worry about your mama. Even when I'm gone, I'll watch over you and make sure you're safe."

Sarah nodded, wiping tears from her cheeks. "Thea says you're going to live in Heaven."

Rebecca dipped her chin. "As we all must one day. But I'll never stop thinking about you, my sweet girl."

"Then it will be just me and Thea and Grandpapa."

Rebecca's arms tightened around Sarah. "I need you to promise me something. Can you do that?"

Sarah nodded, her small brows furrowing.

"Never let your grandfather see your magic. And when you're old enough, leave this estate. Get as far away as you can. Do you promise?"

Sarah bit her lip, considering the request seriously. "Grandpapa is bad, isn't he?"

Pain pierced Rebecca's heart. The last thing she wanted was for her child to be afraid in her own home, but if she lied, this could be Sarah's fate one day, too.

"He wants magic. If he knows you have it, he'll try to take it. You must keep it secret."

Sarah's brow crinkled as she considered carefully before saying, "I promise."

CHAPTER 25

Simon

Dawn was approaching, and the moment Simon had dreaded most was nearly upon him. Since becoming the thing he was now, he'd never trusted a soul with his body while it lay unattended. On the estate, he'd barred the room with his twisted magic, knowing no one could bypass it.

In this foreign land, he'd found creative places to hide, and every day, he returned to it, hoping he wouldn't find his body ravaged by beasts or buried beneath the earth. Being buried alive once was enough to haunt him for the rest of his existence.

Now, he would be forced to rely on eighty-nine men with his secret.

"Williams. Come here a second."

Williams slid beside him along the dark wall of a shipping container.

"I had hoped we'd be aboard a ship before morning, but it's not looking like luck is on my side. For this next part, I'm going to need your help."

Simon looked over his shoulder at the men sleeping slumped beside one another. They'd slept in far worse conditions, and after a night of running and very little food, they would need rest if they hoped to make it home.

He swallowed, the words sticking in his throat. "I... I'm not... Well, you see..."

Williams clapped him on the back. "I know you're not human."

Simon froze, going preternaturally still.

When he said nothing, Williams went on. "You only come around at night. You move too fast for a human, and sometimes your eyes glow in the dark. It wasn't hard to guess."

In five years, no one had seen what he truly was. No one had seen his odd behavior apart from Rebecca. But even she hadn't seen his eyes. He'd begun to believe no one ever would.

Simon stared into Williams' eyes, searching for the same glow, but seeing nothing. "What... What are you?"

Williams laughed. It was a deep belly laugh that settled some of the tension in Simon's taut limbs. "I'm a witch."

Simon slouched against the shipping container. Rebecca was a witch. Alexander was a witch, and it wasn't as if he'd ever asked Alexander what he looked like. Could witches see him as he truly was? Was he this way because *he* was a witch?

For a moment, he dared to hope Rebecca would become like him when her strange illness took her. But that made little sense.

"What gift do you have?"

Williams looked beyond him to the sliver of light cresting along the horizon. "If I'm right, we don't have time for this. Wasn't there something you wanted to ask me?"

Simon dipped his chin. "Yes. We have little time. My... essence leaves my body when the sun rises. I'll need you and the men to bring me aboard and find a place to store my body until nightfall. Can you handle getting everyone aboard?"

"Should we put you in a coffin?"

A shudder rolled down Simon's spine. "No. Find something else. Anything else."

Williams nodded. "I'll get them aboard, and you."

Simon felt it the moment before he left his body and hoped they would be safe for the day.

He rose from the edge of the river and stalked for the cave mouth. Elizabeth was there, and he let out a little sigh of relief. These past several months, he had seen less and less of her. On most days, it was of little concern, but today he had questions.

"Elizabeth, good to see you."

She looked up from her place on the ground and smiled. "Simon!"

He settled beside her, trying to puzzle out the shape she was drawing in the sand. "Is it a dog?"

She stuck out her bottom lip. "It's an elephant."

"Oh. Very nice."

She gave him a look that said she didn't believe the compliment for a minute.

"So listen, I was wondering what you know about witches."

She wrinkled her nose. "You mean like us?"

"What do you mean us?

"You're a witch, and I'm a witch. Are you asking about you and me?"

"No. Maybe. I didn't know you were a witch."

She looked up, setting down her stick. "Well. I guess I'm not anymore. Now, I'm like this." She waved a hand down her body.

Simon considered her words, thinking of how best to phrase his question. "Do you think witches can see this new version of us because we *were* witches?"

She giggled, resuming drawing in the sand. "You're silly, Simon."

He sighed, leaning against the stone at his back. Perhaps it *was* silly to think a child would have answers to his questions.

His thoughts drifted to the night before and what might await him upon his return.

After they'd breached the forest line and were free of the landmines, they'd crossed the road quickly and found themselves in Barth, a small German town overrun by soldiers using the port to bring in goods from all across Europe.

Only one ship per day left Barth, stopping in Demark to unload shipping containers to be sent to the other German-occupied ports. Had he been alone, he would have traveled over land, but with a group of men, many of whom were still weak from illness and starvation, a ship was their best option.

He closed his eyes as the shift happened, and suddenly, he was jarred to life as his world rocked violently.

Around him, men were huddled together in the dark; many had their arms wrapped in thick rope and were hanging on for dear life. He spied Williams and moved to his side, grabbing a bit of rope to keep from sliding across the shipping container's slick surface.

"What's happened?" he yelled over crackling thunder and the waves crashing against the ship.

"We didn't stop in Denmark. We have no idea where this one's going!" Williams yelled back.

"Stay here. I'll go have a look!"

He twisted the bars until the door latch lifted and pushed it open, slipping out of the container. A gale of wind caught the door, swinging it wide as a wave crashed over the ship's deck.

The sky was dark with clouds, and rain pelted him at a severe angle. The ship continued to rock violently as smaller containers crashed into one another.

Grabbing the railing, he bent into the wind, making his way to the bridge. He wrenched the door open and was thrown against the wall as another violent wave tilted the ship dangerously.

Peering through fogged glass, ice ran down his spine as wave after wave crashed over the water, each more enormous than the last. It was evident the crew had abandoned ship some time ago.

He left the bridge, going back to the cargo container where the men were still huddled inside. He swung his arms in a wide circle, beckoning them to follow. They linked arms and slid across the space until they reached the open door.

"Follow me and hang on!" he shouted, and Williams nodded, leading the men over the deck. A wave crashed against the ship's side, and someone screamed as the world tilted before the boat slammed down onto the water, righting itself.

All eighty-nine men made it to the bridge and filed in, Simon pulling the door shut behind them.

Inside, they watched as the dark sky somehow grew darker, several men folding their hands in prayer while others wrapped their arms around handholds, trying to stay upright.

A man, Thomas was his name, retched in the corner. Several others followed.

Simon watched helplessly as the men who had survived more than twelve months of torture fought for their lives yet again.

Tendrils of pre-dawn light clawed their way through thick mist as morning approached. Simon gazed around the bridge at the luckiest group of men he'd ever known. They were tired, cold, and smelled awful, but they were alive.

"Can you see if anyone knows how to navigate this ship?" he asked Williams, who was looking a little green around the edges.

"We're a group of sharp-witted men. By the time you return, we'll be on English soil."

Simon nodded, a new sensation creeping over him. The magic that bound him was fighting for control; it didn't like where he was going. His last thought before he left his body for the day was to wonder why he hadn't felt it pulling him before.

CHAPTER 26

Simon

Simon rose to a smell that nearly had him gagging. He stepped around piles of drying vomit and out onto the deck. Men had shirts wrapped around their heads, arms, and legs, staring listlessly at the flat line of aquamarine encircling them.

Finding Williams, he stopped beside him. "No luck navigating?"

Williams shook his head. "These men are army soldiers. They don't know the first thing about navigating by sea. We've been taking turns watching for land and headed in a straight direction, but we saw nothing all day, and we haven't found water." His voice was strained, and his shoulders were a line of tension.

Simon trailed his gaze across the endless blue horizon, searching for any sign of the direction they should be heading. The men wouldn't last long without water, and their bandaged bodies had injuries that would fester if untreated.

"We need to divide the duties between the men. Some should be tending the wounded, others scouting, and some can search below decks for food or water."

Williams leaned into the railing. "Did all that today. We found ten cans of beans and a shitload of rifles. No water, no medical supplies. The men ate the beans. They were already so hungry."

The need to go left was a pressing ache in Simon's skull, making it difficult to concentrate. It was possible going in the opposite direction would lead them to safety, but it could also mean days of drifting at sea. Days the men didn't have.

"We should go that way." Simon pointed toward the invisible destination he was being pulled to.

Williams didn't argue. He turned, barking orders at several men, and soon, the ship was turning, moving in the direction Simon was so desperate to go.

On their new course, the pressure in his skull eased, and he took a deep breath.

Night stretched on, and men found places to settle down to sleep as Simon watched for land. He feared their new heading even as every hour brought relief from the oppressive hold of Alexander's magic.

Late into the night, something flashed in the dark.

"Brown! Come quick!" Brown and several other men gathered beside him as a glittering port came into view, and several men hugged one another in relief.

They were tired, dehydrated, and needed medical attention, but they would reach land before dawn, and it was the best outcome Simon could have hoped for.

As they approached, a boat raced to meet them. The group waited to be boarded, sagging against one another.

As the first man stepped aboard, rifle over one shoulder, his red armband came into view. Everyone on deck froze.

CHAPTER 27

Rebecca

Sarah's birthday was in less than three weeks. Rebecca had mustered the energy to go downstairs and sit with Sarah in the garden. She'd sent Thea to order a cake and find a nice new dress, and gradually, her heart was mending from Simon's loss.

She was weak, but slowly, she was finding the will to live again. With it, came a renewed determination to take Sarah away from this place and keep her safe. Thea had said she would go with them, but Rebecca hadn't told her yet that she didn't have the money to pay her.

Rebecca could buy anything she wanted on her father's credit, but when she left, she would be cut off. It was a problem she hadn't found a solution to yet.

Sarah danced around her in a circle, creating ladybugs and dragonflies, small birds and butterflies.

"That's very good, Sarah," came a voice several yards away.

A chill ran down Rebecca's spine; she didn't need to look up to know who had spoken.

"Come here, baby." She motioned for Sarah to stand behind her.

Alexander stalked toward them, and Rebecca opened her hand, forming a ball of fire. He stopped, eyeing her magic as it crackled just above her palm.

"I see you're not too weak to perform your little tricks," he sneered.

She let the ball of flame grow, feeling the warmth of her flame lick along her fingers. "You won't touch her."

Alexander peered around Rebecca. "Come to your grandfather, child."

Sarah poked her head out before ducking behind Rebecca's skirts.

"Leave Sarah alone."

"I haven't had new essence in weeks. I need energy, daughter."

Rebecca straightened. "I won't let you use her."

He crossed his arms, giving her an appraising stare, and Rebecca squeezed Sarah's arm, silently warning her to stay behind her.

"I had assumed your magic was used up," Alexander said more to himself than to her. "I never would have agreed to that bargain with Simon if I'd known."

His name, coming from Alexander's lips, twisted her heart painfully, but she lifted her chin.

"Enough foolishness. Give me the child." He lunged for Sarah, but Rebecca flung her flame at him.

The ball of blue sailed harmlessly to the ground, and some of her steely resolve faltered. Once, her flames were magnificent. Once, she would have torched him where he stood.

Now, the drizzle of magic she wielded was pathetic.

Alexander laughed but didn't reach for Sarah again. "Very well. If you prefer, I will take what I need from you."

Rebecca swallowed, glancing behind her at her dark-haired girl, whose eyes had gone round with terror. "Be my strong, brave girl, okay sweetheart? I want you to go to my room and lock the door. Don't open it for anyone but me. Can you do that, sweet girl?"

Tears formed at the edge of Sarah's lashes, but she nodded, her lip trembling.

Rebecca wrapped her arms around her, squeezing tightly. "You are my sweet, beautiful angel, and I will come straight up after I help your grandfather." She squeezed her tighter, pressing a kiss to her cheek. "Go."

She released her, and Sarah ran for the house, not looking back.

Rebecca straightened, and Alexander beckoned her to follow. He turned, not looking back, confident he had her, sure she would do as he asked now that he knew Sarah's secret.

CHAPTER 28

Simon

Simon slapped a hand over his mouth to stop the sound from escaping his lips as another of his men was sent to his knees. The gun cracked, sounding through the night.

He was a coward, hiding while the men were dragged off the ship and lined up. One by one, they gave their name, rank, and unit. As each man gave the information, he was forced to his knees.

He had thought there would be time, assumed he could find a way to save them. But everything had happened so fast. Now, only thirty-three of the men were left, waiting their turn to die.

Each watched as the man in front of him took his place. Resignation and defeat hung from their drooping shoulders.

Even knowing they would die, not one of them had given him up.

The hairs on the back of Simon's neck prickled, and he sensed him the moment before he appeared beside him.

"Sssimon."

Simon wiped a hot tear from his cheek, ignoring the demon beside him.

"Alesssander bid me bring you home."

"I haven't brought him his one hundred demons. I can't go home."

"He sssent me to assissst."

"I'm done helping him."

"It appearsss to me you are exactly where you musssst be to complete the tasssk."

Simon glanced sideways at the insubstantial form beside him, swiping his eyes again. Another shot rang through the air as he glared at Astaroth. "I have come no closer to a solution now than I had a year ago."

"We will transsssport the demonsss in the bodiesss of the dead."

Simon started. "What do you mean?"

"The war isss over. Your friendsss are going home." Astaroth's gaze darted to Simon. "In boxesss."

Something tore in his chest. Some vital part of him wrenched in two. "How?"

Astaroth hovered beside him, seeming to consider his words.

Simon swallowed the bile threatening to rise in this throat. "Demons need live bodies."

Astaroth gave him another appraising look. "We have someone helping on the other side."

The next shot startled him as he leaned into the wall. They had looked up to him, trusted him, but Williams had been something more. He had found a place in Simon's dead heart. His friend slumped to the ground beside the others; a piece of Simon's humanity fell with him.

Simon would have asked: *Why these men? How?* But all his questions suddenly felt irrelevant.

There had been no shortage of death in the year he'd spent abroad. He had watched as countless skeletal men were worked and starved until they took their last breath. He had seen innumerable horrors at the hands of monsters and watched as the last of those he'd tried to save took their final breath.

There was only one person left alive who cared for him: Rebecca. The only thing that mattered now was getting back to her. Suddenly, it felt vitally important that he go home.

"What do I need to do?" His voice was flat, even to his ears, but he couldn't muster the energy to care.

CHAPTER 29

Rebecca

Rebecca held a hand above her eyes, shielding them as she watched fire rain from the sky. Massive balls of flame hurtled toward the earth, crashing into the ocean.

All along the beach, people lounged, sunning themselves, laughing, watching their children chase seagulls. But along the horizon, a dark line surged forward.

"Run!" Rebecca screamed. "Get out of here!" She ran toward the people on the beach, shouting at them, but no one seemed to hear. No one saw the tidal wave racing for the shore.

Rebecca gasped as she clutched her chest. A weight sat on her, making it hard to breathe, and her throat was raw, as though she had truly been screaming as she slept.

"Mama?" Sarah rubbed tired eyes, blinking over at Rebecca.

"It's nothing, baby. Just a bad dream," she croaked.

Sarah closed her eyes and was asleep again in moments.

Rebecca watched the steady rise and fall of the girl's chest, letting it settle her own racing heart. She wasn't sure if the pounding in her chest was because of the dream or the memory of her father's latest experiment.

Since resuming his practice of stealing magic from her, he hadn't given her a night off. In three weeks, he'd found her every night and called her down to his dark table to extract more of her life force.

She was sure now that was his goal. He was draining her life to extend his own.

She closed her eyes as a single tear rolled down her cheek. She would never see Sarah grow up or become the woman she was meant to be. Fear seized her as she thought again of how her father might use Sarah as he had used her.

If only there were a way to protect her.

When Rebecca opened her eyes again, daylight streamed through her window, and Sarah was gone. Something prickled along her skin. A premonition of something to come. Nervous excitement thrummed through her veins, giving back some of the energy her father had stolen.

"Sarah," she called.

Sarah danced into the room, twirling in a new blue dress. "Look, Mama. My new dress is here."

"That was supposed to be a present." Rebecca laughed as Sarah twirled in circles.

"It *was* a present. Today is our birthday!"

Today? Had so much time passed already? She felt as though she had merely blinked, though time had flown by.

"I have a present for you, too," Sarah said, lifting her arms for Rebecca to scoop her up.

Rebecca lifted her, sighing in relief as the strength she always felt at Sarah's nearness bled into her and set her down beside her on the bed. "You do? Where did you get it?"

"Close your eyes, Mama."

Rebecca closed her eyes, holding out her hand. Something solid and cold was placed in her palm.

"Okay. Open!"

Rebecca opened her eyes and gazed down at a small pink stone carved in the shape of a butterfly. "Sarah, it's beautiful." She turned it over in her hand, feeling its solid weight. Not an illusion. It was real. "Where did you get this, sweet girl?"

"Simon gave it to me."

"What?" she gasped as her chest constricted painfully.

"Last night when he came to see us."

Rebecca sat up in bed. Her heart was pounding dangerously fast, and it was a struggle to breathe. "Simon was here? Last night?"

Sarah nodded, growing serious. "He said you're going to be okay."

"Would you give Mama a minute, Sarah?" She choked on the words, holding in her sob.

Sarah hopped from the bed, skipping out of the room. "Get dressed for our birthday party, Mama!" she called from the hallway.

Rebecca swung her legs over the side of the bed, wincing as sharp needles stabbed her heels. She took one unsteady step, then another, and slowly the tingling subsided.

She stopped in the doorway, panting. "Thea. Thea!"

Thea came out of the room across from hers and rushed forward. "Rebecca, you shouldn't be out of bed."

"Help me downstairs, Thea. I need to go to the servant's hall."

Thea wrapped an arm around her, and together, they went down the stairs, stopping so Rebecca could catch her breath at the bottom. When they reached the kitchen, she sat, setting the small pink butterfly down on the counter.

When Rebecca was breathing normally, she stood, waving off Thea as she moved down the hall to the room that had been empty for more than a year.

She rattled the knob. *Locked!* Her heart jumped in her chest. "Alice! Can I have the key?" she shouted in her scratchy voice.

Alice appeared from her room and produced a key, fitting it into the lock. She jiggled it a few times. "That's odd. It's stuck."

Rebecca slapped a hand over her mouth, holding in her squeal.

He was alive!

CHAPTER 30

Simon

Simon opened his eyes, half expecting to be back in camp, thinking he must have dreamed that he had returned the night before to find Rebecca and Sarah asleep in their beds. Not that he could dream in this state; he merely moved from one place to the other.

He had been so tempted to wake her, wrap her in his arms, and bury his face in her hair, drinking her in. But the sight of her, waxy and pale, had made him think better of it. And some part of him was terrified of what she would think of him now. He was not the boy who had left her.

On his long voyage home, beside the bodies of the men he'd called friends and the demons so cruelly stowed away in their bodies, he had more than enough time to consider all he'd done. Would Rebecca love this man—the one who made deals with devils and stood by while friends died? Could he ever love himself again?

He had thought he was a monster before. Now he knew what the word truly meant.

Eighty-nine men, stacked in their coffins, waited for Alexander to claim them. The eleven soldiers unlucky enough to be chosen to complete Alexander's demand had marched back to the estate without a word. Whoever was helping on the other side seemed to control the demons inhabiting them as well.

Once Alexander had taken what he needed from the soldiers, he would bring a few of the men's bodies home each day until he had retrieved them all. It was one benefit of being a wealthy shipping magnate in a small port; he paid a few men to look the other way until he could safely move his cargo, and once he was done with them, they would go to their loved ones to be mourned.

Simon slid out of bed, feeling strangely out of place in the small room. It was nicer than any of the places he'd stayed recently, but it was quiet, and the smell was different—that surprised him the most.

Moving to the door, he curled his fingers into fists and watched as the wood around the edges of his door bent back into shape. It was all he was capable of in his new form.

Twisting the handle, he pulled the door open and jumped back as something flew at him. Roses and fresh apples assaulted his senses as dark hair was flung into his face.

"Simon! You're alive!" Rebecca peppered his neck with kisses as she hugged him.

He was paralyzed for a moment, frozen in place as every part of his being came alive at her nearness. Inhaling deeply, he wrapped his arms around her waist and pulled her close, reveling in the feel of her in his arms.

He had dreamed of this a thousand times, hunched under tree branches in the rain, sloshing through mud, sitting with the men as they talked of the women they hoped to return home to.

He squeezed tighter.

Rebecca gasped, and he released her, pressing her back to look at her. Her skin was pale, dark circles lining her eyes while her colorless lips sucked in air.

"Rebecca."

She waved a hand at him, taking shallow breaths. He could hear the erratic thump of her too-faint heartbeat.

"Rebecca, what's wrong?"

She caught her breath, the color returning to her lips, and her heart slowed a fraction. But not enough.

"You were squeezing a bit tight," she said between breaths. "I'll be fine."

Simon pulled her into the room, sitting beside her on the bed, watching intently as her cheeks regained some of their color.

"I can't believe you're alive," she said when her breathing was under control.

"Why did you believe me dead? Apart from the obvious." He tried to smile, but it died on his lips, weighed down by the heaviness he hadn't been able to shake since that horrible night in Amsterdam.

"Father told me you died more than a year ago. I never should have believed him."

"You never received my letters?"

She curled her hands into fists. "Letters? Father must have kept them from me."

He said nothing, watching for any sign her father had told her the rest.

She lifted her hand, unclenching her fingers, and rested her palm on his cheek. "You seem... different."

He nodded, swallowing.

"Where have you been?" Her tone was innocent enough.

"I went to the war."

A hand flew to Rebecca's mouth. "You were a soldier?"

"No."

Her gaze darted between his eyes, waiting for him to say more. When he didn't, she asked, "Why did you go?"

"Alexander required demons."

Rebecca shuddered. "The job you do for him at night."

"He ordered me to leave and not return until I brought back one hundred demons."

Rebecca gasped. "And did you?"

He nodded.

Throwing her arms around his neck, she said, "Oh Simon, my father is the most cruel evil man. We have to leave. We have to get out of this place."

He buried his nose in her hair, drinking in her scent. "Rebecca... I can't."

She released him. "We must. He has used you terribly, and he will use Sarah next."

"I found a way to stop him from hurting you. I can stop him from hurting Sarah."

Rebecca bit her lip, the flesh between her teeth going white. "He did stop... for a time, but he resumed experimenting several weeks ago."

Rage burned through Simon as he looked her over, truly seeing how weak she had become in his absence. He shot to his feet, tearing down the stairs and flinging the door to Alexander's lab wide.

"You broke our agreement."

Alexander looked up from the corpse on the table. "You forget yourself, Simon."

"We agreed you would not experiment on Rebecca any longer."

Alexander returned his attention to the table. "You broke the agreement first."

Simon's lip curled. "I could hardly bring you two demons per night when you sent me across the world to get you one hundred."

"Not my concern."

Simon moved, but not fast enough. "Simon, stop."

He was frozen in place, several feet from Alexander. Alexander looked down his nose at him as he struggled in vain to close the small distance and end him.

"There's a new darkness in you, boy. Perhaps it is you who are too dangerous for my daughter."

The light glinting in Alexander's eye was the only warning Simon needed, and his stomach dropped. "No," he breathed.

"Simon—"

"No, please."

"You will not see, speak to, or write to Rebecca—"

"No, I'm begging you."

"—for one month. That should be an ample reminder of who answers to whom."

"Alexander. I've been gone more than a year. I brought you your hundred demons. Please don't do this."

"Simon, leave my sight and don't return until I call for you."

Simon spun on his heel, his feet marching him up the stairs. When he was far enough for the magic to consider the instructions fulfilled, he screamed his frustration and raced out the door into the night.

CHAPTER 31

Rebecca

Rebecca heard the front door open and slowly stood, leaving Simon's room and making her way to the foyer. The door was flung wide, darkness swallowing the space beyond. She stepped onto the porch and squinted as she scanned the inky dark.

"Simon. Simon!" Her voice cracked, and she leaned against the doorframe.

When he'd raced from the room, it hadn't been hard to guess where he'd gone, but her strength failed her when she'd tried to follow, to tell him to stop.

Her heart beat painfully in her chest. She feared her father's wrath, but if he'd only been sent on an errand, perhaps he hadn't been so reckless as to confront Alexander. An errand was the least terrible thing her father could have done to him.

Sighing, she shuffled through the foyer and started up the stairs. She would wait for his return. This time, nothing would keep them apart.

Rebecca slid her legs over the side of the bed, letting her feet rest on the cold floor. Simon hadn't returned last night. She'd waited until her eyelids were leaden, giving in to the pull of sleep just as the sun's bright rays burst from the horizon.

She'd slept most of the day, and it wouldn't be long before Simon rose for the evening.

Dressing quickly, she crossed the hall to Sarah's room and smiled fondly at the girl as she stacked blocks in the center of her room.

"What are you building, sweet girl?"

Sarah hopped up. "Mama!" She ran to Rebecca, flinging her arms around her legs and squeezing. "Can we go to the garden? Thea wouldn't take me. She said it's too late."

Rebecca patted Sarah's back. "Yes. It's a fine evening. Shall we bring a jar and catch fireflies?"

Sarah nodded enthusiastically.

Smiling, Rebecca held out her hand and together, they descended the stairs. Sarah waited as her mother moved slowly, catching her breath at each floor.

When they reached the kitchen, Sarah ran to the pantry, found an empty jar and a bit of cheesecloth and string, and brought them back, handing them to Rebecca. As they left the kitchen, Rebecca glanced toward the door leading to the servant's hall. It wasn't quite dark, but she longed to see him.

Just another hour, she reminded herself. When Simon rose, he would find them in their favorite spot.

They settled beneath the oak tree beside the orchard and listened to the buzz of creatures preparing for the evening.

As the streaks of orange streamed between branches and the forest beyond their manicured cage came alive, Rebecca inhaled deeply. Twilight was her favorite time of day—when the scalding rays of sunlight banked and the world melted into the moon's cool embrace. Long shadows stretched the most benign objects into something magical, and imagination was all that was needed to transport them to a land far different from the one she occupied.

Buzzing started, and Sarah hopped to her feet. "Mama," she whispered.

Rebecca smiled, nodding as she slowly stood. "They're waking."

Sarah grabbed her jar and cloth and dashed into the orchard, swiping the jar at the tiny glowing insects in her path.

Rebecca laughed, leaning against the tree at her back.

Sarah's cheeks were flushed and pink as she darted between trees, swinging her arms wildly, but try as she might, her jar was dark.

Rebecca glanced over her shoulder toward the house. Simon should be up, but he had not come to find them. Frowning, she turned back to Sarah, who huffed in frustration as she missed another bug.

Pushing off the tree, Rebecca moved toward her and held out a hand. "May I?"

Sarah considered for a moment, then handed over the jar.

Rebecca squatted down and nudged Sarah's shoulder. "What if we cheat a little?"

A wide grin broke over Sarah's face, and she nodded.

"But this time, I want to see how long we can make them last. What do you say?"

In answer, Sarah cupped her hands together, and Rebecca held the jar upside down over them. At Rebecca's nod, Sarah opened her cupped hands, and a dozen tiny insects flew into the jar. Rebecca slid the cloth over the bottom before flipping it.

"Did you imagine them living a long time?"

"I imagined they would live forever. Just as I pray you will, every night."

Something sharp pierced Rebecca's heart. She had been wrong to tell Sarah what would happen to her; that impending end plagued the girl's thoughts. She could have spared her this bit, at least.

"Come on, sweet girl. Let's take our new nightlight inside. They will chase away the darkness while you sleep."

"I'm not afraid of the dark," Sarah said, sticking her chin out.

"You're very brave. Perhaps they are for me then." She winked, swallowing the fear that rose at the thought of how brave Sarah was becoming and what it might mean for her future.

"You're not afraid of anything, Mama."

Rebecca pasted a smile across her face. If only that were true.

CHAPTER 32

Simon

Simon halted at the foot of the stairs. He tugged at the leash restraining him, but no matter how he pulled, his feet would not turn him in their direction. Gritting his teeth, he tried thinking of some other reason for going upstairs.

The window latches needed to be secured. Alice required his assistance.

Nothing worked. He was rooted to the spot.

He opened his mouth, but words died on his lips.

Alexander's spell was as binding as all the others. Unbreakable.

He turned, spinning on his heel. With Alexander occupied and Rebecca out of reach, he was at a loss for what to do. He went to the kitchen, sitting at the butcher block table, and drummed his fingers over the wood. He could eat.

Standing, he moved to the refrigerator and pulled the door open. Inside, there were several plates made in preparation for the next day. Alice would be sorely upset if he touched those. Sliding a few dishes to the side, he found stew carefully parceled into several bowls for staff. He grabbed one, along with a spoon from the drawer.

He should heat the stew, but as he bit into a cold potato, it was almost comforting, reminding him of nights beneath the tents when a fire would have drawn too much attention, so they ate their meals cold.

Pain twisted his gut as he swallowed. None of the men he'd shared those meals with would ever eat another cold meal. They didn't have the luxury of spoons and prepared meals. They wouldn't crawl into a bed at the end of their night.

He bit into a cold chunk of meat, grinding it between his teeth. It was dead and devoid of the life-giving blood the other half of him craved. The juxtaposition between two warring desires within him, often left a foul taste in his mouth when he indulged one or the other, but tonight, he craved something iniquitous.

It was a reminder that everything about him was wrong.

A startled gasp from the door had him spinning in his seat. Elation soared through him a moment before it was dashed.

A woman stepped into the room. They hadn't met, but he'd seen her with Sarah the night before and assumed she was the girl's nanny. It was a change he hadn't expected to find upon return since Rebecca never let Sarah out of her sight. Or she hadn't before he left.

"You scared me. Why are you sitting alone in the dark?" she asked, a slight quiver in her voice.

"I apologize. I didn't mean to frighten you. I sometimes forget to turn on the lights."

It was a weak excuse for his night vision. Had he been in a better state of mind, he might have thought of something more clever to say, but the words were out, and he could see she wasn't any less unsettled by them.

She flipped on the light. "There. That's better."

Remembering his manners, he held out a hand. "I'm Simon."

She came into the room and took it. "Thea."

She released his hand and moved past him, opening the refrigerator door and pulling out a bowl of stew.

As she moved around the kitchen preparing to warm her meal, an idea wiggled its way into Simon's mind. "Thea, could you give Rebecca something for me?"

She stirred her food, nodding. "Do you have it now? I believe she's still awake. I could take it up after I eat."

"No, I'll be right back."

Abandoning his cold stew, he raced to his room, pulling out paper and pen. He pressed the pen to the page but couldn't form the letters. Biting off curses, he tried again. The pen snapped in two, and he swore again.

Damn Alexander. He was always a step ahead.

He stood, pushing back his chair, and marched back to the kitchen.

"Nevermind. I couldn't find it."

Thea gave him a quizzical look but said nothing as she blew on her spoon, not meeting his gaze as he slid into his chair. She ate quickly and silently before she slipped out, leaving him to his thoughts. There was a loophole somewhere in Alexander's commands. He just had to find it.

With nothing to do with his time and no one to spend it with, he did something he hadn't done in more than a year: he thought of Elizabeth and offered her the use of his body for the rest of the night.

CHAPTER 33

Simon

Three nights had passed, and he was growing restless. Alexander had given him no tasks, knowing it would be all the more torturous when he couldn't go to her, couldn't write to her, couldn't see her.

He paced the long hall lined with windows, hoping for a glimpse of Rebecca, but as with every other night this week, when she moved, he did too. As she breached the treeline, his feet took him in a new direction, forcing him into one of the empty rooms on the first floor.

He didn't bother opening his mouth, knowing no words would leave his lips if she were within hearing distance.

As she moved up the stairs, he listened, Sarah giggling at her side. They talked of their late-night adventures and their latest catch.

He smiled to himself as Sarah chattered incessantly about June bugs and their mating habits. Her sentences ran together, and she hardly stopped for breath as she changed subjects.

"Do you think our fireflies are still alive?"

"Only one way to find out," Rebecca said.

Her voice was like music, capturing his soul and setting it fluttering. He would never grow tired of it. He strained to hear them as they reached Rebecca's room and closed the door.

Invisible bindings released him; he left the room, moving into the now-empty hall.

Three nights of pacing halls and staring blankly at nothing had reminded him that he should be focused on helping Rebecca escape her father. That began with raising enough money for her to leave.

Returning to his room, he reached under his desk for his hidden box and pulled it free. He withdrew the money he'd saved before he left for Europe and stuffed it in his pocket. One hundred dollars wasn't enough for anyone to live on. Once she had enough to set herself up somewhere, he could bring her more.

He picked up his hat and coat and left, stepping into the hall.

Thea jumped back. "I'm so sorry."

"It was my fault," he said, sliding the hat onto his head. He moved to step around her.

"Wait. I have something for you. I was just coming to leave it in your room." She held out a folded piece of paper. "Rebecca thought you were out."

"I'm just leaving. Please tell her—" He pursed his lips. "Nevermind. Have a good evening."

Thea's forehead creased, but she nodded, leaning into the wall as he passed.

He reached the foyer and tore the letter open.

Simon,

I know you must be on one of Father's errands. I pray this one does not take you away from us for another year, but know I'll wait. I'll wait as long as my body allows.

I hope we will meet, but should your time away extend beyond my limited time remaining, please know that I love you. I have only ever loved you, and I will carry you with me to whatever awaits after.

I pray we will be reunited one day, whether in this life or the next. And although you've only been gone three days, I fear I must write this down. One never knows how much time they truly have. You may think me selfish, but if there's one thing I've learned as a mother, it's that you must face your fears and plan for all eventualities.

With this in mind, I ask that you promise me to look after Sarah. Thea is wonderful, and Sarah adores her, but only you know what my father is capable of. Only you can protect her from him.

I hope you return and we escape this place together, but in case my fate is imminent, I'm leaving this letter in hopes you'll never have to read it. But if you do, please do more for Sarah than I did for myself. Don't let my father use her as he used all of us.

With all my love,

Rebecca

Simon folded the letter, sliding it into his pocket. A tear slid down his cheek. She was giving up, but he wouldn't. His soul was lost; his life ended. All that mattered was helping Rebecca and Sarah.

He opened the door, stepping out into the night.

He would do what he must to ensure they were safe.

CHAPTER 34

Rebecca

Rebecca rubbed tired eyes and yawned. She'd woken less than an hour ago and already wished to crawl back into her bed. It had been two weeks since Simon had returned and nearly the same amount of time since she'd seen him.

She had dared to hope he was back for good this time, or, at the very least, they would have had more than a few stolen moments together. But hope was a fickle thing, and it died when not tended. With hope gone, so too had her strength left her.

"Mama, look!"

She looked up, pasting a smile on her face. "Wonderful, darling."

Sarah dropped beside her, pressing a hand to her cheek. "Are you not well, Mama?"

A bit of energy rushed through her, reviving her, and she sat up straighter, resolving to be present for her daughter. She pulled Sarah's small fingers free and lifted her wrist to her lips, kissing the small birthmark shaped like a star.

"I have the same birthmark; did you know?"

The change in subject worked, and Sarah glanced down at her wrist. "Really? Let me see."

She tugged Rebecca's sleeve back and rested her small wrist beside her mother's. Two light brown stars, identical but for their size, stared back at them.

"Wooooow."

A giggle escaped Rebecca's lips. "We are very alike, sweet girl."

A gentle breeze caught the low-hanging branches of the tree, sending a cascade of leaves falling down on them, and they both laughed as they got to their feet.

Rebecca's legs were solid beneath her, and she marveled at the strength that had returned to her, seemingly from nowhere.

"Will you sit for a portrait, Sarah? I haven't painted you in some time."

Sarah wrinkled her nose. "It's *boring*," she groaned.

"What if I promise you ice cream after?"

Sarah's eyes lit up. "Okay!"

"We'll need to move indoors. I need my things to paint you."

Sarah nodded, and, hand in hand, they went back to the house.

Rebecca nearly collided with Thea as she stepped into the foyer.

"I have a letter for you," she said.

"Oh, from who?"

Thea's gaze fell to Sarah. "It's from Simon."

Rebecca's brow furrowed as Thea handed a folded piece of paper to Sarah.

"That's odd," Rebecca said, holding her hand out to Sarah. "Let me see."

Sarah tucked the letter under her arm. "No."

Rebecca pursed her lips. "Now, Sarah, wouldn't you like me to read it to you?"

Sarah crinkled her nose in consideration before handing the letter to Rebecca.

"Come, let's go to the living room." Rebecca unfolded it quickly, scanning it.

Sarah trailed her as she moved into the room and read to the bottom of the page. She should have known. Her father was always up to something. But leave it to Simon to find a way around it.

Sarah climbed onto the seat beside her.

"He says hello, and that grandfather has been naughty."

Sarah nodded seriously, running a hand absently over a cobalt velvet armrest.

"And that he's been staying in the house, but he can't see us for another two weeks. So in the meantime, we must make do with his letters."

"Did he say if he was bringing us a present?"

Rebecca laughed. "He did mention a present. He's working on something for both of us, but it won't be ready for a while. Maybe another month or two."

Sarah frowned, her lower lip jutting out. "Two months is a long time."

Rebecca ran a hand over Sarah's raven curls. "We must be patient for the things that matter most to us. Good things always take time."

She folded the letter, sliding it into her pocket.

"Hey! That's *my* letter," Sarah protested.

"Would it be alright if I held onto it for you?"

"Put it somewhere safe. It's my first letter."

Rebecca smiled, tugging Sarah's curl. "I'll keep it very safe." She leaned over, kissing Sarah on the cheek.

They went to the studio Rebecca had taken over, and Sarah sat with her arms folded over her lap, staring absently at the wall. Rebecca arranged her paints and brushes, sitting down in front of the easel.

As she worked to capture every small detail of Sarah's perfect cherub face, the girl yawned loudly and blew out a loud breath.

Rebecca's lips quirked as Sarah tugged a curl and twisted it around her finger before yawning loudly again.

"Come, it's time for you to get to bed, sweet girl."

"What about my ice cream?"

"Tomorrow. I promise."

When Sarah was tucked into bed, Rebecca pulled out the letter, inhaling its lavender scent.

She read it again.

Her first thought was to storm into her father's underground room and confront him, but Simon's words were clear: the month could stretch into something far worse if they pushed him. They would wait. In the meantime, he was working on a plan to help them escape.

She paced her room. Could they truly leave? It was the answer to her prayers. Sarah would be safe, and she and Simon could start a life together for however long she had.

She read the letter a third time. Soon. Soon, they would leave and never come back.

CHAPTER 35

Simon

Simon tossed his cards down on the table. "Nineteen!"

The dealer turned his cards over. "Seventeen. Player wins."

Simon swiped up a pile of bills as a round of cheers went up around him. That was three in a row—he'd more than tripled his money tonight.

Large men in black suits were pushing through the crowd of onlookers. His sign to go. He flipped his hat onto his head and tipped his chin to the girl serving drinks. She blushed, smiling coyly.

The men closed in. Simon backed up, ducking behind two men vying for the seat he had just vacated.

When he cleared the crowd, he moved faster, rushing out the back door and into the alley. Just twenty-three short blocks away, he stopped at the hidden door to another gambling den. New York City was full of them, and he had enough time for one more stop tonight.

He knocked three times, paused, knocked again, then knocked twice. The door slid open, and a large man appeared. "No."

Simon's smile fell. "What do you mean, no?"

"Boss says. No. You ain't welcome here."

"Come on. My money spends just as good as any other."

"We wouldn't know, would we? We never kept none of it."

The door was slammed in his face before Simon could say more.

It was the third gambling den tonight that had refused him entrance. His luck was drying up. After several weeks, he had enough for Rebecca and Sarah to set themselves up somewhere. The month restriction Alexander had set had expired, and there was nothing keeping him in New York any longer.

Just one thing left to do.

He crossed the street and darted into the night, stopping on the doorstep of a brownstone when he reached Jersey City and knocked.

The door swung open as Thomas Green peered out into the darkness, fully dressed even at the late hour.

"Thomas," he said, stepping past the man into his home.

"What brings you here tonight, Simon?" His clipped tone suggested he had been waiting for another caller.

"I can keep you safe from demons, Thomas, but the men you make deals with at an hour like this aren't my area. I hope you're not up to anything too nefarious tonight."

Thomas shuffled behind him, muttering something under his breath about Simon being one of those nefarious men.

Sitting in the living room of the man's cramped home, Simon eyed the dated furniture, wondering what the man spent his illicit money on.

"What can I do for you? I have other business."

"To the point. It's what I like about you, Thomas." Despite the praise, Thomas frowned. "Right. I'm here because I need you to create two false identities for me. When it's done, I'll need your help to fill out paperwork for a rental property."

"I'm an attorney, Simon, not a smuggler," Thomas answered. "What makes you think I can procure false identities for you?"

"I know the kind of people you deal with, and I'm sure I'm not the first to make this request."

A scowl crept onto Thomas's face.

"Might I remind you, you owe me your life," Simon continued, "and a person who goes back on that can't expect to be saved from a demon twice."

"Very well. I'll need their photos and fifty dollars. Each."

Simon nodded. "I'll pay you when I pick them up. When will they be ready?"

"I need two months."

"Not soon enough. Have them ready in two weeks."

Thomas scoffed. "There is no way—"

Simon stood, letting some of the darkness he kept hidden from the world bleed onto his face as he crossed the room and pulled Thomas to his feet. The man wriggled in his iron grip.

He pressed his nose into the man's face. "I may have saved you once, but if you aren't useful to me, I'll call them here to collect you myself."

Thomas shuddered, knees buckling as he sagged in Simon's hold.

Perhaps he had played the villain a little too convincingly because the terror in the man's eyes only confirmed his own worst fears about himself. But for Rebecca, he would be the monster. He would follow through on his threats.

"T-t-two weeks," Thomas stuttered, and Simon released him, letting him fall to the couch.

He left the room, putting distance between himself and the man whose lingering scent of fear clung to him.

The smell chased him even as he raced through the night, making his way back to Rebecca, the only person who didn't find him repulsive.

He reached the estate, slipping in through the back door, and stopped in his room only long enough to remove his hat.

In the doorframe of Rebecca's room, he watched tiny insects bang against the glass, their bodies lighting briefly before going dark. They cast strange patterns over the walls as they fought to escape.

His attention drifted to Rebecca and Sarah, both curled on their sides. He dropped to the bed, running a finger lightly along Rebecca's hairline, brushing stray curls from her face. Light danced over her pale skin as it blinked on and off.

His chest ached as he watched the tiny creatures fight for freedom, their efforts useless. "Soon," he whispered. He returned his gaze to Rebecca's serene face. "Soon, I'll free you both."

CHAPTER 36

Simon

Simon rose, and his gaze went to the bulge in the side of his coat pocket. Elizabeth had called him a fool for leaving it there for anyone to find while he was gone for the day. He'd told her of his earth magic and how it was a twisted thing since he'd been changed, how he'd used that twisted gift to secure the room while he was away.

She'd shrugged and said people found ways around magic all the time.

With that unsettling thought in mind, he moved to the coat, pulled the money out, and spilled it across his desk. It was all there. Nearly one thousand dollars. After he paid for their identities, their tickets to New York, and the apartment, there would be enough left for them to live on for at least six months.

It was plenty of time for him to win more money for them. Though New York gambling dens were closed to him, he could find others in every major city.

Scooping the money up, he pulled the box under his desk free and stuffed it inside before securing it back in its place. Then, he turned his attention to the door and pried it open.

Moving swiftly, he raced up the stairs and caught the edge of the doorframe as he stopped in it, exhaling slowly.

Rebecca was sitting up, face angled away from him as she stared out at the full moon. Silvery light framed the left side of her face, making it appear ethereal. Truly, she was breathtaking.

"Rebecca."

She turned, her whole face lighting up as her eyes met his. "Simon."

She reached for her blankets, but he crossed the room and pressed her back into the pillows, cupping her face in his hands as he pressed his lips to hers.

She opened her mouth, sucking in his bottom lip, and he groaned as he leaned into her, his tongue sweeping the inside of her mouth.

A sharp intake of breath had him lifting off of her. "I'm sorry. Did I hurt you?"

His gaze traveled over her face, lingering on swollen lips before their eyes met.

She sucked in another breath, and he released her, sliding back off the bed. "Rebecca, what's wrong?"

"I'm just"—she inhaled sharply— "struggling to catch my—"

Simon pressed his palm gently against her breast. Her heart was racing, galloping in her chest, but it wasn't the thundering of a strong heartbeat. It was erratic, and he had never been more terrified.

Sitting lightly on the bed, careful not to press any weight into her, he helped her sit up.

She smiled up at him, but it was strained.

"Has your father been experimenting? I had thought he'd be distracted. With all the..." He let the words die.

"I'm just glad you're here."

Her words set a range of emotions alight within him. He wanted to storm downstairs, gut Alexander where he stood, and watch the life drain from his vile corpse, but Rebecca was so frail she might topple over if he wasn't holding her up.

He slid back against the headboard and sat perfectly still as she leaned against him. Her breathing was shallow, coming in small pants, and even as her heartbeat slowed, it grew fainter. How had she deteriorated so rapidly?

If he had been there to stop Alexander from draining every ounce of life from her, she wouldn't be in this state.

He slid an arm behind her and shifted so she could face out the window.

"Simon?"

He angled his head toward the door. "Hello, Sarah."

She skipped into the room but stopped when she saw her mother.

Rebecca beckoned for Sarah to come, and the girl started forward again. She climbed onto the bed beside Simon and leaned into his other side. Finding her mother's hand, they laced their fingers over his lap.

"Mama," she said, staring at the full moon hanging low outside the window, "are we leaving now that Simon's back?"

"Yes, sweet girl. We will start packing tomorrow."

Simon's gaze dropped to their clasped hands, and a sharp pain sliced through him. She was lying to Sarah as he had intended to lie to her.

Rebecca knew her time was nearly up.

They stayed like that through the night, and Rebecca and Sarah nodded off a short time later. Simon leaned his head back, watching the moon's slow descent as he counted each of Rebecca's heartbeats against his chest. Each time it stuttered, pausing before continuing its laborious task, fear seized him.

Each time, he thought it might not start again.

Sarah curled onto her side, mumbling something and tiny butterflies appeared in the room, blue and iridescent. They circled lazily over Rebecca's head and expanded until cerulean flapping wings circled all three of them.

As orange glowed along the horizon, Simon studied Rebecca's face, memorizing her features and hoping desperately she would still be with them when he returned that night.

CHAPTER 37

Rebecca

Rebecca struggled to peel her eyelids open, finding the effort entirely too taxing. She tried again, blinking in the blinding false light. Peering around the room, she realized she was sitting up, reclining against a warm, solid form.

She pressed a hand against Simon's chest, smiling. He had stayed the night with them, trusting them to care for his body when he left. It was the first time he had spent the night with her. She twisted, curling on her side and wrapping her arms around his still form.

In that moment, she longed for nothing more than to feel his arms around her, too.

Sarah stepped through the door, holding a basket full of flowers. "You're both lazy."

"Sarah. That's not polite," Thea said, stepping in behind her. Her cheeks flushed pink as she took in the pair on the bed. "I'm so sorry, Miss Rebecca. I didn't realize..." She looked away and reached for Sarah, turning her around.

"No, you're fine." She sucked in a shallow breath. "Please, come in."

Thea looked scandalized for a moment, but she released Sarah, letting her run to the bed. "I brought your flowers, Mama. Simon, wake up!"

She shoved his still form and frowned. "What's wrong with him?"

Rebecca tried to push herself up, but her arms shook, and the bit of effort it took to try had winded her. "Thea," she panted, "give us... a minute."

Thea backed out, closing the door behind her.

"Sarah... listen... to me." Rebecca patted the bed, giving herself a moment to catch her breath. "You need to pack. We're leaving tonight, sweet girl."

Sarah nodded, poking Simon's arm. "Is he dead?"

Rebecca choked on a startled laugh and wheezed through the pain spiking through her chest. "No. He has to"—she sucked in a breath—"go away... during the day."

Sarah wrinkled her nose and shrugged. "Okay."

Rebecca reached out, finding Sarah's hand, and squeezed. "He's going to take us... away... tonight. Will you... pack... for me?"

Sarah nodded.

"Good girl. Go... pack."

Sarah slid off the bed, leaving her basket of flowers behind. "I picked those for you. Love you, Mama."

She bounded from the room, throwing the door open as she left.

When she was gone, Rebecca closed her eyes, trying not to focus all her attention on the myriad of aches riddling her body. She let herself imagine she would go with them. They would find a cute house in Chicago, far from her father and his demons.

She and Simon would raise Sarah as their own, take new names, and live out their days together. In her imagination, he would get a job, and rather than being in some in-between place all day, he would be at work, and each night, he would come home and greet her with a kiss.

They would dance by the fireplace, listening to their favorite songs. Then, they would slide into bed, and she would rest just like this, against his chest, falling asleep in his arms.

A tear slid down her cheek, and she didn't have the energy to wipe it away.

"How sweet."

Rebecca's eyes flew open, heart hammering in her chest. She turned her head as her father crossed his arms.

"Crying for your life? Or your lover's?" he taunted.

"Leave him alone," she gasped out.

"He's not your husband, Rebecca. While I draw breath, you will not share a room with a man you aren't married to. Even if he is half a man."

"He's more... man... than... you."

Rage danced in her father's eyes, shooting ice down her spine. He lunged forward, gripping Simon roughly by the arm, and yanked him off the bed. Rebecca fell back, hitting her head on the headboard.

"Stop," she cried. "You'll... hurt him."

He didn't spare her a second glance as he grabbed Simon under the shoulders and dragged him backward out the door. She heard the thud of Simon's shoes as they clacked against the stairs.

She rolled over, crying out as pain shot down her left arm; she fell over the side of the bed, landing hard on the floor.

"Simon," she cried uselessly, pulling herself across hardwood planks. Her chest constricted painfully as she gasped for breath. Her head throbbed, but she slid her hands out in front of herself and reached for the bedpost. "Simon," she breathed.

Her skin was hot and cold at the same time, and the room was spinning. She closed her eyes, relaxing her head on one side, letting the cool wood soothe her flaming cheek.

A light breeze ran over her face, and it felt like the caress of fingers along her skin. In that moment, her pain vanished, replaced by a comforting calm.

Rest, light, a deep voice she had never heard whispered in her mind. *Soon, you will be free of this suffering and this life.*

She nodded—or thought she did, but her body felt weightless. Maybe that was just her mind floating above her body.

I don't want to die alone, she thought.

You're not alone. I have been with you from the moment you were born, and I will be with you for eternity.

CHAPTER 38

Simon

Simon opened his eyes and knew something was wrong. His heels ached as if they had been struck repeatedly, and the ceiling he was staring at was most certainly not Rebecca's. He sat up and gazed around the dining room. It was a space no one used in this house, and he couldn't imagine how he'd ended up here.

He stood, dusting his pants and jacket as dread bled through him. Stuffing his hand into his pocket, he pulled out a folded sheet of paper. He unfolded it with shaking fingers, already knowing who it would be from.

You still think you can outsmart me. I would ask when you'll learn, but I imagine it will be too late when you do.

He crumpled the letter into a ball in his fist, seething.

"Mama?"

The small voice coming from the fourth floor caught his focus, and he darted up the stairs.

When he reached Rebecca's room, he stopped, staring at Sarah, who was wiping tears from her eyes. Moving around the bed, a pale hand was the first thing he saw before the rest of Rebecca's still form came into view.

He dropped to his knees beside her.

"Rebecca... Rebecca, wake up."

He touched her wrist, already knowing there would be no pulse. Leaning, he pressed trembling lips to her forehead, feeling her cool skin against his mouth.

Pain tore through him as he lifted her into his arms. She was so light. So frail. He wanted to hold her close and never move from the spot, content to petrify wrapped around her, shielding her from the world the way he never could when she was alive.

A small sob shattered the frozen moment, and he looked up at the girl wiping tears from her eyes, attempting bravery for a mother she didn't understand was already gone.

Slowly, he stood, moving toward Sarah. Each step away from Rebecca tore at the gaping hole in his chest. He wrapped Sarah in his arms, lifting her, and squeezed her gently.

"It's okay," he whispered. "You will be okay."

It was a lie. Nothing would be okay ever again.

He moved blindly, taking the stairs two at a time as Sarah wrapped her arms around his neck and wept. Her small chest rose and fell as tears ran down Simon's collar and onto his skin. He had been wrong to assume she didn't understand.

In that moment, he remembered the letter, knowing her wishes. She wanted him to take Sarah and go. Get her as far away from Alexander as he could.

"Simon. Put my granddaughter down."

Simon's arms loosened as he bent to set her on the floor. She squeezed his neck tighter, not releasing him.

"Simon. I said release her." There was a bite to Alexander's tone that promised violence.

He tilted his head, whispering in Sarah's ear. "You will okay, but you'll have to let me go for a moment. Do you trust me?"

She squeezed tighter but, after a moment, nodded her head, and her arms fell to her sides.

Simon turned to face Alexander, and Sarah laced her fingers through his, facing him as well.

"Come here, Sarah. I am your grandfather. That man is not your family."

Her tears had dried, and the small girl squared her shoulders, reminding Simon painfully of Rebecca.

"No."

Alexander's jaw clicked as he bit down on unsaid words. He swiveled his gaze to Simon. "Bring her to me, Simon."

Simon's legs moved mechanically, dragging Sarah behind him. She stumbled to her knees, but he was forced to keep walking. Agony twisted through him as she began to cry again, tearing her hand from his.

She turned, running from them, and Simon's body moved, chasing after her.

When he reached her, he scooped her up, and she fought like a feral animal to get out of his hold. "Please, Sarah, stop fighting me. When I bring you to him, I'll run so he can't use me. But you have to give me a chance to get away."

She stopped fighting, small whimpering noises escaping her as he reached Alexander and set her down.

He ran the moment her feet hit the floor, as fast and as far as he could, not stopping until he was in town.

He slouched against a wall, dragging in ragged breaths. Images of Rebecca's limp form raced through his mind, burning the backs of his retinas.

As long as he existed, he would never forget the press of her cold skin against his lips. The silence that surrounded her like a shroud. Where the love of his life had been, only a shell remained, her once vibrant laugh snuffed out by the cruel machinations of her father.

A sob burst from his chest. She was gone. His reason for being had died before he could free her. He had failed her.

He had failed them both.

CHAPTER 39

Sarah

Sarah dug her heels into the floor and scratched at her grandfather's arm as he pulled her along. Seemingly unaffected, he continued down a set of stairs she'd never seen to a room wholly new to her.

In the dark, she glanced at shadowy outlines of the same terrifying creatures surrounding the estate. When he released her, she dropped to the floor, crossing her arms over her chest.

Alexander glanced down at her and sighed. "I know we haven't gotten to know one another well, Sarah, but let me make something clear. I am your only family now. You will listen to me, or life will be very difficult for you."

Sarah's bottom lip quivered as her mama's still form flashed in her mind. She blinked several times and swiped at her eyes.

"There, there, child. I just need to get a few things straight, and I'll send you right back to your nanny."

He opened a book and set it on a dark table at the center of the room. Pulling a necklace from around his neck, he waved a hand, and a ball of orange engulfed it, lifting it over the table. As he began reciting words from the book, Sarah's mind grew fuzzy, her vision blurring.

She yawned loudly.

A noise from across the room startled her, and she and Alexander both turned as Simon strode in.

"Alexander."

Her grandfather opened his mouth to speak, but Simon interrupted. "No. It's my turn to talk."

Alexander closed his book, facing Simon fully. "Very well. Speak."

"You may have the ability to control me with your spells and tricks, but there will come a day when you'll need me, and you'll have to rely on my goodwill."

Alexander raised a brow.

"I have a deal to make with you." He glanced down at Sarah, and she blinked away her tears. "You will never harm a hair on Sarah's head. Never use her for any of your experiments, never put a spell on her. And when that day comes, I will save you without coercion."

"I have Astaroth for that. Sarah is valuable to me."

"If you think the day I speak of isn't your pet demon turning on you, you're more fool than I thought."

Alexander glanced at Sarah, then back at Simon. "If you want me to keep a promise like that, I'll need more from you in return."

Simon nodded. "Finding two demons a night is unsustainable, as we both know. But I will promise three demons per week for the rest of Sarah's life—or yours, whichever comes first. But if you break our deal, so will I."

"You're already bound to me. Why should I agree to this?"

"You can have a life with my willing participation or one that's as difficult as I can make it. And if I find a way to end myself, I promise you I will."

Alexander uncrossed his arms, darting another look at Sarah. "Very well. She doesn't have much magic, anyway."

Simon nodded, crossing the room, and the two men clasped hands.

Then, before Sarah knew what was happening, Simon had scooped her up, and the world blurred by. They stopped in Thea's room, and Simon set her down gently.

Thea tore her sheets aside and met him in the middle of the room. They whispered, and she staggered back against her bed. Simon's quiet words, still unclear to her, were sharp, and Thea nodded.

He knelt, meeting her eyes, and kissed her forehead. Up close, she could see the red rimming his amber eyes. "Sarah. I need you to be brave. Your grandfather has promised to treat you well, but if that ever changes, you must tell me or Thea immediately."

Sarah blinked several times and nodded.

"Good. I'll be back. Stay with Thea, okay?"

He stood, turning to go.

"Simon."

He turned back. "Yes, Sarah?"

"Bring Mama outside?"

He dipped his chin, meeting her stare, and disappeared.

THE END

EPILOGUE

Simon peered up at the woman staring out her bedroom window, and his breath caught. After seventeen years, there was no denying their likeness. Sarah was only two weeks shy of twenty-three, and every time he saw her, there was a moment of hope.

Then she would smile or open her mouth to say something kind or sweet, and that hope died.

She had never known the cruelty and horror Rebecca had experienced, and it was a glimpse of who Rebecca might have been under different circumstances. Somehow, she'd forgotten everything from her childhood. It hurt knowing so few people carried her memory after she was gone.

Thea had often said it was the mind's way of protecting itself.

But when Sarah's child had been born, around the same time as Thea's, he was certain some of their fondest memories would return to her. He'd even seen Sarah and Claire catching fireflies.

She may not remember, but subconsciously, those memories were buried in her mind. He wanted to shake her and ask her why she was suppressing memories of the woman who had given everything for her.

Helping her remember had become his obsession.

He would leave a small trinket out for her to find or mention Rebecca casually. Most of the time, she rolled her eyes at him or gave him a playful laugh and continued with her day, but occasionally, he saw a glimpse of something in her eye. It was as though, for a moment, it had come back to her, but then that blank stare was on her face, and he knew he'd only imagined it.

Simon stepped into the Graves home and closed the door behind him.

"Good, you're just in time," Sarah said, laughing. She hoisted Claire onto her hip and handed him a glass jar. "Come with us."

He twisted the handle of the door he'd just come through and ushered them out. As he followed Sarah, watching her dark curls sway in the moonlight, another stab of pain shot through him.

She stopped under the oak tree where the three of them once sat and was hit with déjà vu. Suddenly, it was 1942, and she was Rebecca, holding Sarah.

"How can you remember none of this?" he demanded, spinning to face them.

Claire burst into wailing sobs, and the moment shattered. Claire was nothing like quiet, observant baby Sarah. She was loud, and she cried often.

Sarah rounded on him. "What do you think you're doing, scaring her that way?" Her dark brows were slashes across her pale skin, but when she saw his expression, her face softened. "I know you loved her. I know she meant the world to you, Simon. I wish I could remember, but you remember her well enough for both of us."

He sighed, handing over the jar. "It's just that this was your favorite thing to do together. Some part of you must remember."

She set Claire down in the grass and smiled. "Come catch fireflies with me. Claire prefers to chase the beetles."

He nodded and followed Sarah into the orchard. As he trailed her, another pang of longing hit him. She raised her jar into the sky, and a firefly landed on its edge. Just this once, he let himself imagine that when she turned, it would be Rebecca who looked back at him.

The firefly rounded the lip of the jar, and she slid a bit of cloth over the top, turning to him and grinning in triumph. The air hitched in his lungs, and she was so like Rebecca he longed to fall to his knees and beg her to forgive him for never freeing her from that jar.

"Firefly," he breathed.

The smile on her face faltered. "What? What did you say?"

He lifted a hand, gently touching her cheek. "Rebecca was my firefly. I never set her free. I never got to keep my promise."

Sarah stepped back, and the jar in her hand crashed to the ground. She brought her hands to her head and shook it, staggering back.

"Sarah." Simon moved, wrapping his arms around her waist as she sank. "Sarah, what's wrong?"

"Simon?"

"I'm here. What can I do?"

She blinked and stared around the orchard. Her gaze drifted to his, and then she screamed, clutching her head again.

"Sarah. Sarah. Please, tell me what's wrong."

Memories of Rebecca's pale form stretched across her floor raced through his mind as he squeezed her tightly, terror gripping him. Her body was trembling in his arms, and he relaxed his hold.

"Please, Sarah."

Slowly, the trembling stopped, and her hands fell to her sides.

She gazed up at him, a fog clearing from her vision as recognition lit up her eyes. "Simon."

"Yes, Sarah. Are you alright?"

"Simon." She lifted a hand, touching his face. "It's me. Rebecca."

THANK YOU

Thank you for reading Firefly. If you enjoyed it, please consider leaving an honest review on your favorite site. If this is your first foray into the world of the Prophecies of Angels and Demons, consider starting at the beginning with Grave Secrets. To read Grave Secrets and the entire Prophecies of Angels and Demons series on Amazon

POAAD Series
Amazon Links

Leave a Review on
Amazon

CASSANDRA ASTON

ACKNOWLEDGMENTS

If you've made it this far and kept reading, a special thank-you to you. Readers like you give me the courage to keep writing and keep telling my characters' stories. If you loved this novella, please consider leaving a review. Your words of encouragement are sometimes exactly what I needed to get through my day.

To my mom, who continues to be my first reader, even the horrible first drafts, I'm so grateful our love of reading brought us even closer.

To my son, who tells everyone he meets about my books, sometimes to my embarrassment. Thank you for being my biggest supporter.

To my street team, for believing in me and being so willing to give your time and energy to share my stories with the world.

To Dawn Darling for being a great friend and sounding board.

To Michaela C for being such an amazing editor!

Thank you.

www.ingramcontent.com/pod-product-compliance
Lightning Source LLC
Chambersburg PA
CBHW021200130626
46554CB00005B/1903